The Mohawk Showdown

Twenty years after being jailed on a trumped-up charge of train robbery, Jack Garrison escapes from Yuma Penitentiary with nothing to his name but an old banjo and the hope of proving his innocence.

Jack is banking on the help of his younger brother, Rick, to wreak revenge on the true villain. But the person who masterminded the robbery is determined to remain undetected, pulling many strings to protect his identity. His influence puts a violent end to Rick's help, and Jack's old friend Joe Dublin also pays with his life. Fighting for survival, Jack finds an ally in blacksmith Ed Corcoran, as they go head to head against the true villain in a violent climax.

The Mohawk Showdown

Matt Laidlaw

A Black Horse Western

ROBERT HALE · LONDON

ISBN 978-0-7198-1803-5

Robert Hale Limited
Clerkenwell House
Clerkenwell Green
London EC1R 0HT

www.halebooks.com

Printed and bound in Great Britain by
CPI Antony Rowe, Chippenham and Eastbourne

PROLOGUE

Phoenix, Arizona

He was at the roll top desk when she walked into his home office. The room was lit by an oil lamp with a deep red glass bowl, a matching silk shade. He had been sitting there deep in thought, staring at the various pigeonholes stuffed with meaningless papers, documents, the ink pots with their quill pens – and, inevitably, alongside the blotter a bone-handled revolver with an intricately engraved barrel.

He had seen none of that. His eyes had been on inner thoughts, his mind involved with a particular problem to which there seemed no easy solution. It had been the unconscious drumming of his fingers on the desk's oak top that had drawn her to the room.

She was tall, elegant, with dark hair worn in a chignon, and a plain long dress that might once have been expensive but was now quite old and well worn. She sat down gracefully, crossed slender legs and arranged her skirt modestly as she reclined in the overstuffed easy chair. Her gaze when she looked at him was cynical. Her eyes were ice-blue.

'I used to believe,' she said conversationally, 'that the position of councillor was a reasonable first step on a very tall ladder. But that was a long time ago. How old were we, Jeff?'

He swung his swivel chair to face her. He was a big man with black hair and even blacker eyes. His white shirt showed patches of damp at the armpits. His black trousers were shiny at the knees.

'I've been a town councillor for ten years,' he said. 'We were both thirty.'

'And now we're forty,' she said, 'you're still on that first rung and I'm bored, and impatient. Jefferson T. Rome. It really does have an imposing ring to it. But a name's just a name, Jeff, and I'm a woman who needs much more than that.'

'If what you're saying is, "I need more than that, or else", then forget it, Ella. Don't let impatience overrule those reliable instincts that made you marry me. Your choice was correct; I'll go so far as to say it was inspired. You see, I've looked at exciting possibilities, and reached a decision. Tomorrow I set the wheels in motion.'

'I'm intrigued. I want you very close to the political summit, but to get there you need influence, or money. My dear, you have neither.'

'I'll get the money. Everything else follows.'

'What are you going to do, steal it?'

'There's no other way.'

'Really? I thought you'd done with that life? I know you had made quite a name for yourself, acquired a reputation as one of the fastest guns in a land where fast guns are as numerous as grains of sand in a desert. But you gave up all that wickedness when you met me. Turned your back on the owlhoot, became a respected member of society.'

'Nothing has changed.'

'Yet you are considering furthering your career with stolen money.' She pouted. 'I wonder what Tony, our only son, will say when he finds out. A boy of twenty, who's just become a deputy marshal right here in Phoenix.'

'He won't need to find out. I told him of my plans. Our careers will be mutually beneficial. We can help each other, through the good and the bad.'

'Not just theft, then. You're quite willing to corrupt my son?'

'So now he's your son?' He smiled. 'Either you weren't listening, or heard only what you wanted to hear. I told him my plans, and that's all. He will not be involved.'

'My concern is for what might happen to *him* if *you* are caught, and his complicity is discovered.'

'There is no complicity.'

'But he would be classed as an accessory, either before or after the fact, and for that he could go to prison.'

'That won't happen.'

'If it did,' she said, 'you would then have me to deal with.'

For a few moments there was a heavy silence, both of them immersed in deep thought. Rome seemed amused by her threat. She was clearly excited by his startling announcement. Electric tension filled the room. The quiet dragged on for too long, became uncomfortable. It was broken by Ella.

'I'm quite sure you need an awful lot of money,' she mused. 'That suggests a major heist.' She smiled. 'If you're going to be a thief, I suppose I'd better learn the strange language they use in gangster circles.'

He nodded. There was the sheen of sweat on his brow.

'And when it's done,' she went on, 'your hands need to be lily white. A man in high office in the nation's capitol doesn't want skeletons falling out of cupboards.'

'I may handle the money when it's been stolen, but I won't be directly involved in the theft. There was a young man in university who committed a very nasty crime and got away with it. He has that skeleton in *his* personal cupboard, and I've threatened to throw the door wide open.'

'In official circles I suppose they call that delegating.' Again she smiled. 'And you want him to organize some kind of grand theft? Well, if he committed some unspeakable offence then I'm sure he'll do your bidding to save his skin, but when it's done there'll be resentment. You'll be looking over your shoulder for the rest of your life.'

'Give me some credit, Ella.' Rome was shaking his head. 'It's all worked out. The skeleton is the lever that gets me money to buy influence and power. I keep my little delegate and his merry band of robbers sweet by bankrolling them for the rest of their lives.'

'At risk of leaving us short?'

'Bankroll was the wrong term. They'll be paid a pittance.'

'And does this man with a past live here in Phoenix?'

'No. He's many miles away, far enough to ensure that there can be no possible connection between us. A place called Sureño, on the Gila River.'

'My goodness, I know it. So he's a country boy. And his name?'

'His name,' Jefferson Rome said, 'is Elgan Lloyd.'

PART ONE

ONE

Twenty years later

It was late afternoon when Jack Garrison rode down from the Mohawk Mountains on a stolen horse.

He had left Yuma before dawn, pushed hard into the Gila Mountains, ridden a long loop that took him to the south of Coyote Peak and so into the Mohawks. Now, with the westerly afternoon sun casting long shadows, he let the big blood bay pick its own sure-footed way through boulders littering the more treacherous of the steep, arid slopes. At dusk he was out of the foothills and had ridden north. By the last of the sun's fading light he found a spot that took his fancy on the green banks of the Gila River, fifty miles to the east of Yuma.

A helluva long ride to end up too close for comfort to the town that was home to the state penitentiary – but no matter. Distance was not his main concern, and there was speculation in his gaze as he looked back at the purple hills.

On the banks of the river the cottonwoods that in the day provided shelter from Arizona's blistering sun would, at night, retain some of the heat that would otherwise leak away into clear, cloudless skies. The thin blanket rolled behind his stolen mount's saddle would suffice to keep him warm, and the tinkling music of the river would play its part, lulling him to sleep.

But he was getting ahead of himself.

He dismounted, shrugged off the old open-back banjo that had been strapped across his back since the chill light of dawn, and leaned the instrument carefully against a tree trunk. He stripped the rig off the bay, led the horse down the grassy bank to the water's edge and let it drink. Then, leaving it to wander and graze, he prepared his own supper.

He built a small, smokeless fire under the trees. The flickering light from the flames lit the overhanging branches and grey-green leaves, creating a comfortable canopy over a campsite encircled by shadows. Bacon and beans taken from a Yuma general store with a flimsy back door that opened to a push sizzled merrily in the blackened pan he'd found in the roan's saddle-bags. From a new coffee pot suspended over the flames the tantalizing aroma of hot java mingled with the scent of the burning wood. He unrolled the blanket, put the saddle at its head. Found an old log, dragged that to the fire and sat down with a tin plate onto which he tipped the piping hot meal.

Ten minutes later he wiped bacon grease from the empty plate with a hunk of dry bread, ate the bread, and was finished. He moved away from the fire. Looking about him, he unbuckled the stolen gunbelt and hung it from the split stub of a broken branch. With the light from the flames barely touching his boots, he sat with his back against a tree trunk and a tin cup of hot coffee on the grass at his side.

Then he reached for the banjo.

While everything he carried with him – and that carried him – had been stolen, the banjo had been his for almost twenty years. A man had been dragged spitting and cursing from a Yuma cell, and hanged at dawn. The cell was still warm when Garrison was tossed in like a bundle of rags and left to rot. Days later, he had found the banjo draped in cobwebs under the dead man's cot. His playing of the instrument might have driven other prisoners to distraction, but without doubt he knew that over the years the banjo had saved his sanity.

He tapped his fingers lightly on the taut animal skin head scarred by years of use, ran his thumb across the gut strings, tweaked a tuning key and listened to the gentle plinking drift away into the night. Then, banjo in his lap, he leaned back. Down-picking with his middle finger, double thumbing to add a gentle rhythm to old-time, country-style music, he played his own melodic version of *Garrison of Alabama*, then segued into *Oh Susanna*, which he always figured was the same older tune been tinkered with. He leisurely finished the coffee. Half a dozen tunes followed, fast, slow, rhythmic, haunting; his eyes felt heavy; sleep was pulling him down when he picked the opening notes of the *Arkansas Traveller*—

The first bullet sent glowing sticks whirling smokily

from the fire like the first wave of Indian arrows. One landed on Jack's shirt. The cloth began to smoulder. He flapped at it as the second shot punched a hole in the hanging coffee pot. It clanged, swung wildly, brown liquid hissing into the hot embers. The third shot thunked into the tree trunk where Jack Garrison's head had been resting, but he was already gone. Before the echoes of that first shot had faded he had thrown himself sideways.

Then he lay there. The six-gun in its holster was hanging from a tree yards away, out of his reach. His only weapon was the open-back banjo he clutched to his chest. The coffee had dowsed the fire. It hissed like angry snakes. The campsite was ill lit by moonlight filtering through the canopy of cottonwood leaves. On the river-bank the light was brighter. Jack Garrison watched a man dismount from his horse, leave it to wander away to where the big blood bay was standing alert, then come up the slight slope. He was carrying a rifle. Against the luminous silver gleam of the Gila River, he was little more than a dark shape. Stopping by the dying fire, he looked across at Jack.

'Careless,' he said. 'Or maybe downright stupid. Which is it, Garrison?'

'You're calling the tune,' Jack said.

The man laughed. 'The tune is what brought me here. I lost you coming down from the hills, was about to give up until daylight when I heard that damn banjo.'

'So I made a mistake. But what about you? I don't suppose there's any need to ask why you're here?'

'Maybe there is.'

Garrison thought about, then nodded. 'So that's the way it is? I escape from Yuma State Pen. The governor discovers his loss, but doesn't want me back.'

'So far, so good.'

'He doesn't want me back, but neither does he want me running loose.'

'Going places. Asking awkward questions.'

'Questions that might get accusing fingers pointing in his direction? I was one of a gang who robbed a train, stole a lot of money. Innocent guards died. I was caught, and I've been paying the penalty.' Garrison shook his head. 'Appears clear cut, but that's not the way it was, not the way it happened. If the truth came out, heads would roll.'

There was no reply, just an unconcerned shrug. 'You really think I'd get answers, after twenty years in Yuma?' Garrison said. 'Turn the clock back, prove my innocence by finding those train robbers?'

'It's what you think, not me – but none of that matters. When I leave here, you'll be a dead man and I'll have earned my bounty.'

'You're that good?'

'I'm the best. And you're a long reach from a weapon of any kind.'

Garrison looked down at the old banjo that he'd clutched to him as he threw himself away from the bullets. He sat up, climbed to his feet as the attacker tensed, ran a hand over the banjo's strings and smiled. He looked up at the bounty hunter.

'You familiar with banjos?'

'I know they make a helluva noise. Drove the governor to give you a cell all on your lonesome. Close to twenty years, alone with your thoughts and that banjer,' he marvelled. 'No damn wonder you're *loco*.'

Garrison grinned. 'That's just it,' he said. 'Inside, it got me what I wanted, and any banjo man will tell you if the noise gets too much these fine old instruments can be muted.'

There was a metallic snap as the bounty hunter jacked a shell into his rifle's breech. He was about to earn his money, but it was never easy. His face tightened as he closed his mind.

'Look,' Garrison said. He turned the banjo lovingly in his hands so the open back was exposed. 'This here metal bar's what's called the co-ordinator rod. Stuff a sock behind it, a rag, any old bit of cloth' – he pulled a wadded red bandanna out from behind the pitted metal bar – 'and the sound's deadened.' He shrugged ruefully at the bounty hunter. 'So that's what I did when I'd eaten my grub' – he held up the wadded bandanna – 'and I figured once I'd done that the sound wouldn't carry and I'd be safe here for at least the one night ....'

He was holding the man's gaze as he rattled on, keeping the killer's mind at a distance from his cocked rifle and trigger finger, at the same time dropping his hands and casually unfolding the bandanna that had been inside the banjo.

He did it neatly, without haste. The tiny Remington .41 pistol hidden in the folds dropped neatly into his hand. Looking into eyes that dilated with shocked aware-ness, Garrison shot the bounty hunter in the throat, the bullet ripping through the carotid artery.

He watched as the man stayed on his feet for an instant, eyes still wide but swiftly glazing as blood spouted from the terrible wound. Then his knees folded and he fell face down across the fire. The coffee leaking from the bullet-holed pot had killed the flames, but the heat in the embers was intense. The night air was filled with the stink of singeing cloth, of burning flesh.

'Bragging got you nowhere, because you were never the best, and you were wrong about the other, too,' Garrison said. 'I didn't make a mistake, my friend, it was deliberate. I knew there'd be a man on my tail. A pris-oner escaped. The warden liked to keep the lid on lapses in security, and that's the way he always played his hand: better a dead convict than a man free to boast in some run-down saloon bar. So rather than let you waste energy hunting me down, I played the banjo to draw you in – and, goddammit, didn't it work a treat?'

TWO

When Jack Garrison had hurled himself recklessly off the top of Yuma State Penitentiary's high stone wall, hit the ground in a panic, and scuttled like a rat through the undergrowth towards the lights of the nearby sleeping town, he'd possessed nothing but the prison uniform he stood in, and a banjo close to a hundred years old.

At sun-up thirty-six hours later, he set off along the misty banks of the Gila River riding the stolen blood bay and leading the bounty hunter's fine chestnut mare. The mare's saddle and saddle-bags lay hidden under dead leaves beneath the cottonwoods: quick thinking had warned Garrison that no man rides into a town leading a saddled horse without inviting awkward questions.

He had two double eagles, more money than he'd seen in twenty years. The gold was in a pocket of the man's worn leather vest. It was a shade too big for Garrison, but its worn, aged look went a little way towards disguising the newness of the clothing and fine boots he had taken from the Yuma general store's pegs and hangers. Also, in addition to the new Colt .45 and Remington .41 derringer he had stolen from the general store, he now had a spare gunbelt carrying a Remington Frontier .44 with walnut butts worn from being grasped frequently by the bounty hunter's calloused palm. The man had used a Winchester '73 on him when he rode in. That and it's saddle-boot was another addition to Garrison's armaments.

In Garrison's prison cell there had always been a tin mirror, small and buckled and of little use, showing his face in a weird, cracked kaleidoscope. He had washed at the river before leaving the campsite, and his reflection staring back at him from the cold waters of the Gila had damn near scared him to death. His once black hair was shoulder length and streaked with grey. He had stopped shaving ten years into his life sentence. His full, ragged beard and flowing moustaches were also mostly grey, and above the facial hair and the aquiline nose his black eyes glittered like wet stones.

The eyes of a man, he had mused, who was plumb stir crazy, out of his mind, or filled with a raging hope that he could now right the wrongs that had sent him away in chains to endure years of penal servitude.

He was forty-five years old, could have been sixty. And he was amused by the realization that nobody in his home town of Sureño would give him a second glance when, later that day, he rode in to begin the hunt for the train robbers.

THREE

The forge was white hot, its light dazzling in the small workshop. In the intense heat sweat was dripping from the blacksmith's face as he used a lump hammer to shape a glowing strip of metal into a horseshoe. The pall of smoke from the forge hung under the low board ceiling, gradually drifting under the door's lintel and out into the evening sunlight where the big blood bay stood dozing. Sparks flew as the hammer clanged on metal and anvil, raining down on Jack Garrison. He waited patiently, the question he had asked hanging unanswered in the pungent air.

The blacksmith straightened with a muffled grunt. He dragged a meaty hand across his face, spat into the glowing coals, and used tongs to raise the cooling metal and survey his work.

His eyes still intent on the rough horseshoe, he said, 'Rick Garrison, eh?' and seemed to heft the hammer speculatively. 'Who wants him, and why?'

'It's me doing the asking.'

'And you are?' From a fierce face reflecting the forge's glow, bright blue eyes turned to look at Garrison.

'An old friend. We go back a long way.'

'I came here from Phoenix fifteen years ago. Fed up with life in the big city.' He pursed his lips, seeming to appreciate the irony in his description of the state's modest capitol. 'At that time,' he said, 'Rick Garrison was ten years old. Used to fish in the Gila with a bamboo pole and a bent pin. Where were you?'

'Around.'

'Around? Not around Rick Garrison, that's certain, and I'm not too sure you'd want to be around him now.' He paused, appraising Garrison's ragged appearance and filthy, bloodstained attire, then took a breath. 'Or the other way around, if you get my drift. Rick has his standards, so he'll be the judge of that. If you want to risk it, you'll find him over at the jail.'

'Locked up, or…?'

'Or,' the blacksmith said, grinning crookedly. 'For the past five years Rick Garrison's been Sureño town marshal.'

The bay had thrown a shoe as Garrison rode into Sureño. The ride from the campsite to his home town had taken most of the afternoon, and as he pushed the two horses on through the heat of the day his thoughts had been occupied with the difficulties that lay ahead. He was no fool. In his hunt for men who had robbed a train but lived now in a world that had moved on, he would need help. But in the eyes of the town he had been part of the gang, the one man left alive to pay for the crime. For a convicted man now on the loose, help would be almost impossible to find.

Almost. Earlier that day there had been, in Jack Garrison's mind, one glimmer of hope.

He had a brother he had not seen for twenty years. Was he, in the eyes of his brother, sinner or saint? Would his brother help him? Or would he, after one glance at the unkempt, bearded stranger bearing the stink of a prison cell, turn his face away and inform the Sureño marshal that an escaped convict was in town?

Rick Garrison had been five years old when his big brother Jack, manacled but with head unbowed, had been led away to the Yuma stage by two armed guards from the state penitentiary. The brothers were orphans, and for twenty years Jack Garrison had lived with the haunting memory of a saloon bar turned into a court-room and of being watched by two frightened brown eyes set in a pale face; of the stern woman with iron-grey hair who was holding the frightened, tow-headed child's hand; of her thin lips and the weight of her accusing gaze on his back that hot summer's day.

Ten years in, the prison warden had informed Garrison that the woman had died. She had been a distant aunt, so there had been no grief. But when he had asked about his brother, there had been a noncom-mittal grunt from the man behind the desk. The boy was fifteen. He'd get by.

Now, as he rode away from the blacksmith's shop and turned the bay towards the stables where he'd left the bounty hunter's horse, Garrison was acknowledging that young Rick had done much more than get by. Also, that his choice of a profession that demanded he uphold the law was a fine tribute to his character after what had happened to his brother.

But in pinning on a town marshal's badge and taking up office, Rick Garrison had presented Jack with a massive headache. His one slim hope had been nipped in the bud, and at that moment he didn't know which way to turn.

FOUR

Sureño's main street ran parallel to the Gila River, widening halfway along its length into a sizeable square. Late in the day, activity was slackening, with businessmen padlocking their doors, riders heading out of the dusty street to nearby ranches, the plank walks emptying as women shoppers hoisting long skirts out of the dust hurried home to prepare dinner.

The saloon, Mackie's, was set on the river side of the square, between a gunsmith's and a grain store and directly across from the town's jail and marshal's office. When Garrison headed across the square with the banjo slung across his back and the raging thirst of a dying man heading for a waterhole, someone in that office put a match to a lamp and in the warm glow a figure could be seen moving across the window.

Despite his beard and long hair, Garrison felt naked and exposed. He turned his face away and picked up his pace, even though he was pretty sure he had little to fear. Already he had encountered two men he knew, and both had walked past him without a second glance. One of them, now a very old man, was the circuit judge who twenty years ago had handed down his sentence. The judge had looked at him with nothing more nor less than utter contempt for the type of man he saw before him, but of recognition not a flicker had crossed his lined countenance.

The interior of the saloon was cool, dim, reeking of beer, strong spirits, and stale tobacco. What little light there was from high, dusty windows picked out glittering highlights on the shelves of shiny bottles. Men drinking at the bar glanced at Garrison as he signalled to the barman and ordered beer. One, a businessman in a suit, nodded sociably, then turned back to the Phoenix newspaper he was reading. Another, a stocky young man with a deputy marshal's badge pinned to his vest, wore a Colt .45 in a holster hanging from a gunbelt worn tight around his waist. Clearly he was no expert with firearms, had no gunfighter aspirations. His face was flushed, damp with sweat. He looked ill. After one searching look at Garrison, he turned away and continued a conversation with the big man in a leather apron standing next to him.

That man was the blacksmith.

Garrison's drink came sliding along the bar. He had split one of the gold eagles when paying for the blacksmith's work, and had enough small change to take care of the drink. He carried it over to one of the tables standing against the long wall opposite the bar. When he sat down, the blacksmith was watching him. Garrison knew the man must have downed tools immediately after shoeing the bay, and crossed the square while Garrison was with the hostler. He'd probably expected to find the deputy in Mackie's, and the lawman would now be aware that Garrison had been asking questions about his boss, Rick Garrison.

The question was, what would he do?

A man was sprawled in a chair at the next table. Bottles and empty glasses stood in puddles of spilled liquor. He was coughing harshly, sparks flying from the cigarette dangling from his lips. He looked like the town's derelict, the kind of down-and-out who would walk into a saloon when the doors opened and begin cadging drinks. Unshaven, unkempt, his clothes worn and dirty, his appearance was an embarrassment to Garrison because looking at him was like looking in a mirror: he was seeing again the reflection that had glowered back at him from the waters of the Gila.

Garrison washed out his dry mouth with the beer, swallowed the tepid liquid with a grimace. He removed the banjo from his shoulder and sat back. He was despondent. His moonlit scramble over the prison wall and the clean break from Yuma had filled him with elation. The clever ruse that had led to the bounty hunter's death had convinced him that years of confinement had not taken the edge off his intelligence. But, though never previously allowing the thought to surface, he admitted now that there had been a deeper reason for the euphoria: he had always been looking ahead to the day when he would turn to his younger brother for help. Working together, they would find the men who had robbed a train and blown open the secure carriage using dynamite that had killed three of the guards.

Discovering that his brother was Sureño marshal had been a bitter blow. Now it appeared that even his first casual questioning of the town's blacksmith could be leading to a heap of trouble.

Moodily reflecting on life's travails and unfailingly bleak prospects had been a relentless, draining feature of prison routine that drove some inmates to suicide. Garrison had always tackled those problems by turning to the battered open-back banjo. Without conscious thought he was doing the same now. His fingers were absently stroking the strings. The barman had turned from the unending chore of rinsing glasses, and was watching him from across the room.

Because he was in his home town, Garrison's thoughts naturally drifted. In his younger days he had been a harmonica man. Around smoky camp-fires under a canopy of stars, with a *remuda* of twenty or more horses dozing in the rope corral and steers lowing in the velvet darkness, there had always been one request.

'Hey, Jack,' someone would call, 'how's about giving us *Skip to my Lou?*'

He tried it now, on the banjo. Picking the notes with finger and thumb, he closed his eyes and crooned the words under his breath, choosing the verse that summed up his predicament and set it to sweet music:

Lost my partner. What'll I do?
Lost my partner. What'll I do?

Lost my partner. What'll I do?

Skip to my—

The table next to him went over with a crash, sending empty glasses flying. Out of the chaos of shattered glass and broken timber the unshaven derelict hurled himself at Garrison with a howl of anger.

He hit Garrison's table and threw himself bodily across it. A swinging fist cracked against Garrison's cheekbone. The powerful blow knocked him backwards. His head cracked against the wall and he saw stars. Then the man was swarming all over him. Reeking of sweat and beer, he threw a left-hand punch that chopped into the side of Garrison's neck and set him choking. A second right-hand punch mashed Garrison's bottom lip against his teeth. He felt it split. Hot blood coursed down his chin. Dazed, he tried to ward off the next blow and found his hand caught in the banjo strap. The punch cracked against the other side of his jaw and the room dissolved in a red blur.

Then the man's face was tight up against his, teeth bared, breath hot on Garrison's face.

'Don't play that tune,' he gritted. 'Not ever. You play it again and it'll be a gun, not fists, and it'll be the last tune you ever plunk on that goddamn banjer, the last sound you hear in this life—'

Then abruptly he stopped. His face was so close to Garrison's they were nose-to-nose. His big left fist was bunched in Garrison's shirt front, holding him steady for the next blow. But those fingers slackened. The dere- lict's mouth dropped open. He pulled back. His eyes had widened, and beneath his whiskers his face had paled.

'Jack?' he said in a hoarse whisper. 'Jesus Christ, is that you, Jack Garrison?'

Then he was dragged away from Garrison as a hand grasped his shirt collar. The stocky young man wearing a badge had come rushing across the saloon's dirt floor to uphold the law.

The derelict was not finished. 'The old creek, Jack,' he gasped hastily, 'get there whenever you can,' and he twisted to drive an elbow into the lawman's hard belly. But he was the worse for drink and no match for the much younger and fitter deputy. A knee slammed into his back. A strong arm came over his shoulder and he was dragged further away from Garrison in a crippling head-lock. Then, as the derelict bucked against the restraining hold and flailed wildly with his bloodied fists, the burly blacksmith came in from the side. He hit the derelict once, at the angle of his unshaven jaw – and it was over.

'What was all that about?'

'He objected to my playing.'

'I've seen him go wild when the mood takes him, but that was different. You two got history?'

'Tell me his name, and I'll give you an answer.'

'Joe Dublin.'

'Never heard of him,' Garrison lied, and he shook his head. It ached. He dabbed at his face with the bandanna that not too long ago had been inside the banjo enfolding the derringer pistol. He winced as the cloth dragged across his split lip.

31

Dublin was conscious, but slumped in a chair with his head in his hands. The blacksmith had taken one look at him then gone to the bar. He came back, nudged Dublin upright and handed him a drink.

The deputy had a bandanna in his hand. He was mopping his red face. His hand was unsteady, and he was eyeing Garrison with some irritation. 'I expect nothing less from Dublin,' he said, 'but you've got my interest.' He hooked a thumb at the blacksmith. 'Ed Corcoran tells me you were asking about the marshal.'

'The name rang a bell. I thought I knew him. I was mistaken.'

Corcoran shook his head. 'That's not the way it looked. You told him you and Rick were old friends.'

'He convinced me I was wrong.'

'That sounds like someone talking his way out of a tight corner,' the deputy said. 'Another thing Ed says is you clammed up mighty quick when you heard Rick was town marshal.'

'Not true: the blacksmithing was all done, my horse shoed. But, going by appearances I'm an unemployed drifter. Any marshal worth his salt would take one look at me and throw me in a cell.'

'A drifter who pays for my services with a gold double eagle that was clinking against another when you fished it out of your vest,' Corcoran said. 'Rode into town on a fine blood bay. Had a chestnut mare on a lead rope. The six-gun outfit you've got strapped around your waist is so new it's coated with dust from the store shelf.' He shook his head. 'I see long greying hair and whiskers and that tells me I'm looking at an old man, but I'm beginning to wonder what else is under there.'

The drunken derelict called Joe Dublin began chuckling softly, richly, and the blacksmith shot him a glance before again turning to Garrison.

'All the time I was working on your horse,' he said, 'I was being watched by young eyes in this old face, and the pallor of your skin I can see leads me to just one conclusion.' He rubbed his hands down the front of his leather apron. 'So tell me, now, why does Deputy Lynch smell trouble?'

The deputy had been listening intently, and now he seemed to reach a decision. 'Rick's in Yuma, got official business with the prison warden. I could lock you up until he gets back, but he'll be out of town for the next couple of days. You've not broken any law I can name. If Corcoran's right about the horses and those gold eagles, it don't make sense giving you free room and board.'

The unspoken implication in the words didn't escape Garrison: he was being told to leave town. He came stiffly out of his seat, nursing bruises, and slung the banjo over his shoulder.

'So tell your story to the marshal,' he said, 'but, in your own interests, leave me out of it. A grey-bearded old man with two fine horses, who packs a shiny new six-gun and pays for services in gold? Hell, try telling that fairy story to Ricky Garrison when he gets back, and you could be out of a job.'

By the time he'd finished talking, Garrison had worked his way to the door and was out on the plank walk in the warm evening sunlight. He'd half expected to be called back. That hadn't happened. And although the news that his brother was in Yuma talking to the prison's warden should have further dampened spirits that had already been at a dismal low when he walked into Mackie's, for the first time since going over the wall there was now a spring in his step.

'Joe Dublin,' he thought, a half-smile crinkling his eyes as he gazed up at the rich red skies. 'Now who in the world would have believed he'd be the one to step into the breech?'

FIVE

Poco a Poco Creek, several miles to the east of Sureño, came snaking down out of the hills to spread into a shallow pool on a small plateau that would be a little above the head of a tall man standing on the banks of the Gila. Scrub and small trees were watered by the lake thus formed, and from there the creek poured between worn sandstone outcrops and so emptied into the big river.

In an ideal world all that would have been true. But this was sun-baked Arizona, and Jack Garrison could scarcely recall a time when the creek had been anything other than a dry, rocky watercourse without a trace of moisture.

That evening Garrison rode to the creek along a riverside trail bathed in bright moonlight. He still had the chestnut mare on its lead rope. He'd offered it to the Sureño hostler at a bargain price when he left Mackie's saloon, and might have settled for less when the toothless ex-wrangler began to haggle. But there was suspicion in the old man's eyes, and Garrison had backed off. He had the remaining double eagle, and change. Knowing for sure that the next few days would bring a heap of trouble, he could have done with flour, coffee, beef jerky, and extra shells for both six-gun and rifle. But the town's stores had been closed. The dead bounty hunter's Remington .44 was in his saddle-bags, but was an irritation because it meant he had two pistols taking different calibre shells.

He'd kept it with Joe Dublin in mind.

The drunken derelict who had attacked him in the saloon and left him with bruises and a split lip was nowhere to be seen when Garrison reached the creek. His memory had served him correctly: along the river's banks there were several stands of cottonwoods, and the higher ground rose steeply to his right. Knowing that Dublin would be coming from the direction of Sureño, Garrison rode around the trees to the east of the creek. There he hobbled both horses and left them. They were out of sight from the trail, and the hobbles and lush grass would prevent them from straying.

Then, hanging the banjo by its strap from the horn and slipping the bounty hunter's Winchester out of the blood bay's saddle-boot, Garrison clambered up onto the plateau and lost himself in shadows.

As he sat back against the slopes of the higher ground and lit a cigarette, he was thankful for Dublin's tardiness. It gave him time to take stock, to figure out where he went next in a situation that had been turned on its head by Rick Garrison's actions in following in his brother's murky footsteps.

And, in truth, murky was a mild way of describing the dirty dealing that sent Jack Garrison to prison.

Twenty-five years ago, it had been Jack who was marshal of Sureño. He had grown weary of ranch work, walked away from the conviviality of those night-time roundup camp-fires, slipped his harmonica into his vest pocket and moved into town to pin on the badge of a law enforcement officer. Trouble was he was a kid of twenty. He was way out of his depth, and unaware that he had been chosen for the job for that very reason.

Three years in, he had rounded off a month of patient observation by arresting a young man called Lloyd. He'd been caught red-handed rustling cattle. The result had been a two year prison sentence.

But young Geraint Lloyd's father was Elgan Lloyd, a small-time rancher with a big temper which he used to bend people to his way of thinking and gain influence on the town council. Within a week, Marshal Jack Garrison had felt the full force of his anger. Officially, Lloyd could do nothing to change the situation: his son had been led by an older man, but caught cold, and was little better than a horse thief. But unofficially, in a final purple-faced, spittle-flying confrontation in the marshal's office, he had sworn that Jack Garrison would be made to pay.

It took Lloyd two years, and even then it couldn't be proved that he was behind what happened. By then, Jack Garrison had again grown restless. He had handed his badge to an older, wiser man. On the night that his world began to crumble, he had no gainful employment; while not looked on as a loser, it was reckoned by most that he was a man who would drift comfortably through life without making an indelible mark.

On that night that would always be stamped on his memory, four men robbed a train carrying many thousands of dollars in used banknotes across country to San Francisco. They had used felled trees to stop the train, dynamite to gain entry, and three of the guards on the train had been blown to bloody shreds in the massive explosion.

The way legend had it, a posse of grim-faced men rode hard and fast out of Yuma when the alarm was raised. They caught up with all four robbers in the Mohawk foothills when they stopped to rest their horses in a thick stand of blue Palo Verde. Three of the captives were hanged from the tallest of those trees, and left there to rot. The fourth man made a break for it. Somehow, he got clean away. He took the money with him – or so the story went.

Two days later, the Sureño marshal and two hastily sworn-in deputies had ridden up to Jack Garrison's home. In a swift search that took in every room in the house and the ramshackle outhouses on the edge of the property, they discovered bags with government markings. A few crumpled banknotes were inside one of the bags. At the back of a cobwebbed shelf the searchers found several sticks of dynamite.

Garrison was arrested, and charged. It was impossible for him to say where he had hidden the money because it had never been in his possession. But it should have been easy for him to prove his innocence. On the night of the robbery he had been out of town when usually he would have been found propping up the bar in Mackie's saloon, but he'd been nowhere near the railway tracks, which passed a little way to the south of Sureño. He had been on the plateau at Poco a Poco Creek with 17-year-old Joe Dublin, playing five-card stud poker by the light of the moon and a crackling camp-fire and from time to time frightening away the coyotes with the wailing of his harmonica.

One of the tunes requested by Dublin had, Garrison recalled now, been *Skip to my Lou.*

It had been a pleasant evening. The poker had been played for low stakes, a jug of whiskey had been passed to and fro – glistening in the flickering firelight – and there'd been a lot of laughter at bad jokes as the alcohol took effect.

But when Joe Dublin had been questioned twenty-four hours later by lawmen in the Sureño jail, in front of the prisoner, he had sworn on a tattered Bible that he had not seen Jack Garrison for at least a week.

And in an ironic twist to the story, when Jack Garrison was convicted and taken in irons to Yuma State Penitentiary to begin a life sentence for the killing of the three guards, a grinning Geraint Lloyd was walking out of the gates after serving his time for cattle rustling.

'I should have plugged you as you rode in, put a bullet from the '73 through your lying black heart, watched you bleed to death.'

'That's no more than I'd expect, no more than I

deserve,' Joe Dublin said, 'but you'll be the loser. You need me, Jack.'

He was tethering a sway-backed paint pony to some prickly scrub on the small plateau. He'd come riding off the trail as if he knew exactly where Garrison would be waiting. And, Garrison realized, that should have come as no surprise. Hell, without knowing it he had chosen the exact spot where, as young men, they had built their crackling camp-fire from bone-dry chaparral, played cards, drunk their fill of rotgut whiskey, and cracked drunken jokes in the moonlight.

'I need a liar,' Garrison said, 'like I need a hole in the head.'

'You think that's all I did? Lie?'

'You mean there was more?'

'The whole evening was a set up. If you remember, coming out here was my idea. I suggested it, because that's what I'd been told to do.'

'Jesus Christ,' Garrison said. He pushed himself to his feet. His inclination was to vent his anger in violence, knock Dublin to the ground and beat him senseless with fists and boots. But how do you knock the sense out of a man who appears to have none?

Also, a moment's thought told him there was a ray of light in Dublin's story.

'If someone told you what to do, gave you orders,' Garrison said, 'you must have a name, you must know the man, and if you know him—'

He broke off, because Dublin was shaking his head.

'More than twenty years ago, Jack. Besides, whoever

was behind that train robbery isn't stupid. The man giving me orders was himself following orders, probably under threat. He was a range tramp glad of a couple of dollars, a stranger in Sureño. And that's the way it stayed. He was there that day, then gone, never to be seen again.'

'You were a sassy 17-year-old kid with an old short-barrel Peacemaker you were just itching to use. It's hard to believe you were scared by a no account drifter,' Garrison said scornfully, 'so you must have listened to those gold coins jingling—'

'I was a kid with a father lost both legs in the Mexican wars and came home to find he was widowed,' Dublin said, and there was anger in his voice. 'This feller, he said he wasn't alone. Told me his pard was about to take my legless pa's left hand off with a rip saw to show they was serious, would take his right hand off in the same way if I stepped an inch out of line.'

Garrison shook his head. He moved away to the edge of the plateau, gazed down at the water glistening in the moonlight.

'So you lied,' he said, not turning, not giving Dublin the crumb of comfort that might have come from his understanding. 'And because of that, I spent the next twenty years in prison.'

'I'd do it again, if I was over the same barrel,' Dublin said. 'And, now you mention it, what's with this twenty years?'

Garrison swung on him, frowning. 'What the hell's that supposed to mean?'

'You got life, but you're here now so, what, you came

over the wall?'

Garrison nodded.

'Why did you wait twenty years?'

Garrison stared, hearing the question with a kind of numbness, his mind looking for answers he'd sought again and again, but never found.

'Time gets away,' he said hesitantly. 'A man sees the inside of those walls, he hits the depths. If he claws his way back up, five years have gone. Without noticing, all those fives stack up. It's like any raw kid of twenty on the outside who wakes up one morning and realizes he's thirty-five and wonders where the years have gone. That's the way it was with me. Until one day the hated warden retired. By the time the new man with polished boots and a fresh-pressed uniform strutted in through the gates, most of the guards in Yuma were so drunk they couldn't stand. I took my chance.'

'In twenty years there must have been other days,' Dublin said dismissively. 'If you'd made the break sooner you'd have set us both free. You realize that? You from prison, me from guilt – and, more to the point, the trail wouldn't have been cold. We could have hunted them down, those train robbers.'

'A trail's never cold. The Chisholm's not been used since the days of the big cattle drives, but a man can follow it across the prairie easy as a line snaking across his own palm—'

The bullet chopped off his words. It smacked into the rock behind Garrison, sending sharp splinters whining into the night. The sharp crack of the rifle followed a

42

split second later. He was facing the wrong way but on the fringe of his vision he saw the red muzzle flame which pinpointed the gunman's position. Across the river. Firing through the mist rising off the cold water. Then more shots followed in rapid succession as the gunman worked lever and trigger. The paint pony's legs buckled and it went down, a bullet through its brain. There was a cry of despair from Joe Dublin. He turned, and made as if to run to the twitching horse.

'Get down,' Garrison roared.

Acting on his own words he ran to the plateau's edge and hit the ground on his belly. Out of the corner of his eye he could see his frightened horses fighting the hobbles as they left the cottonwoods behind in their efforts to get away from the noise. The bullets were still whistling across the river, chipping rocks from the rising ground behind the paint. Garrison wondered if there was more than one attacker out there. If Dublin had a gun, and the courage to return fire.

He thrust the Winchester forward. Squinting through the hanging mist at the flickering muzzle flashes, he looked across the open sights and planted six fast shots into that distant scrub. The response was silence. No agonized screams told of a mortal injury inflicted, but the gunfire ceased as swiftly as a snuffer kills a candle's flame.

Then Dublin was wriggling up beside him.

'Crazy fools picked the wrong spot,' he said hoarsely. 'Rivers too deep to ford; they'd need to swim their horses across and you'd pick 'em off easy.'

'Why me doing the shooting? Why not you?'

'Never had a rifle. I needed cash, sold my Peacemaker maybe a year ago.'

'You sold your soul and then your gun.'

'For Christ's sake, Jack—'

'Forget it. All that blazing away at us was for show. They figured they might get in a lucky shot, but mostly it was a warning. Listen ....'

The ground was baked hard. They could hear the crackle of scrub and the sound of hoofs, far off and moving away. One man, Garrison reckoned, and wondered who.

'Warning me or you?' Dublin said. 'And how'd they know where to find us?'

'In twenty years neither of us forgot this location, so why should they?'

Dublin was up on his feet, dusting himself off and looking back at the paint.

'I sold my gun, my horse is dead—'

'Keep wondering if I'm soft in the head,' Garrison finished for him. 'I should put that to music,' he said, heard Dublin's chuckle and felt sudden warmth. Harsh words had been spoken, wounds would take time to heal, but they'd been friends and needed each other. He climbed to his feet, kicked away the empty brass shells.

'You got any strength left after seeing off that gunman, there's a chestnut mare down there that's yours if you can catch her. And there's a .44 Remington in my saddle-bags, with gunbelt and shells. Take the rig off your pony, and you're all set.'

'With all that,' Dublin mused, 'I could live my dream and rob banks.'

'You and me both,' Garrison said, 'but I've got a better idea.'

SIX

The rifle bullets had come ripping at them across the river, tearing gashes in layers of thin mist lit by cold moonlight. By next morning the mist had thickened. The cold light of the moon had been replaced by the hot rays of the rising the sun, and Garrison and Joe Dublin had moved away from the plateau at Poco a Poco Creek. They had crossed the river, pushed on, and were looking down from an elevated location further north but several miles closer to Sureño.

They were high enough to believe that they could see Yuma in the hazy distance to the west, Gila Bend to the east.

Their protracted, late night reconnaissance had born fruit.

Garrison had known that Sureño was out of bounds, but that the town had to be at the very heart of their hunt for the train robbers. He had recalled his descent from the Mohawks, and of gazing down and across the distant river to the foothills and high peaks of the Eagle

Tail Mountains. When he and Dublin left the plateau and crossed the river, that was the direction they had taken. A short way up the slopes of the Eagle Tail foothills they came across a blind gully. It was a thirty foot gash cutting across the landscape, with just the one way in and no exit. For the length of its high side a shelf of smooth rock formed an overhang. Horses and men would find shelter there from the heat of the midday sun. The ridge was a deep gully. On its downslope side there was a low ridge of softer earth, with a tangle of parched chaparral and stunted mesquite providing cover but allowing a clear view of the foothills, river and town.

They were all set, Garrison had figured. They had a campsite that was about as safe as they could make it. And, thanks to Joe Dublin's unexpected initiative the night before, they had the name of a man who was going to get unexpected, unwelcome visitors.

When the distant rifleman had packed his bags and ridden off in the moonlight, Dublin had headed at a jog for the edge of the plateau, calling over his shoulder to Garrison that he was borrowing his horse.

Before Garrison could object, Dublin had slid down the slope in a flurry of dry rocks and was running for the edge of the cottonwoods where they had last seen the spooked horses. That put him out of sight. When next Garrison caught sight of him he was up on the big blood bay and riding it down the bank and into the mist shrouding the deep waters of the Gila.

Outraged, Garrison had sworn softly but could do

nothing to stop the man.

Once across the river Dublin had ridden through the scrub to where they'd seen the last muzzle flashes, dismounted, done a quick search, then mounted again and ridden back to the river. They had exchanged words across the misty waters. Garrison had listened, angrily objected, then shaken his head and set to work. He'd stripped the saddle from Dublin's dead paint; done what he could with loose rocks to protect the carcass from scavenging animals; struggled with the paint's rig through the riverside cottonwoods to where the chestnut mare was standing, ears pricked, nervously alert.

Then, on the saddled chestnut, he too had crossed the river,

'Geraint Lloyd,' Dublin had said without preamble. 'Saw him in Corcoran's smithy a week ago. His horse had a broken shoe. He wouldn't meet Corcoran's fee, so that's the way it stayed. There's sign all over the ground. This rifleman was riding that horse.'

'You know where we can find Lloyd?'

'Lives with his pa.'

And that had been that.

From the general store Garrison had plundered in Yuma, he carried two large water canteens. They'd refilled those from the Gila, then swapped mounts and headed north.

Wet pants from the river crossing on Garrison's roan notwithstanding, now astride the chestnut mare and with the .44 Remington hanging low from the waist belt with its filled loops, Joe Dublin had been a man transformed.

The slumped derelict with rounded shoulders and dull eyes had been replaced by a square-shouldered man who exuded an air of confidence. He rode erect in the saddle – his hand frequently dropping to the new pistol as if to reassure himself he wasn't dreaming – and for most of the ride he took it upon himself to lead the way.

At the foot of the Eagle Tail Mountains he had dropped back. Without knowing what they were looking for in the fading moonlight, they had unknowingly ridden into the blind gully and realized it was the ideal campsite. After unsaddling the horses, Dublin had taken one of the saddle-blankets for bedding, and they had settled down to sleep through what was left of the night.

When next Jack Garrison opened his eyes, the new Joe Dublin had a fire going and was cooking breakfast.

'Twenty-four hours ago I was getting lukewarm slop pushed under a cell door,' Garrison said, yawning as he rose and stretched.

'Twelve hours ago I was in Mackie's saloon, punched a man in the face and looked at a ghost,' Dublin said. 'I'm still in shock. Don't ask me what I'm doing, just tell me what we do next.'

'We eat, then we shave.'

'Do that,' Dublin said with a grin, 'I'll be seeing another ghost, this time in the mirror.'

'If we had one,' Garrison said, 'which we don't. But whoever was doing last night's shooting, whoever put him up to it, they have a picture in their minds. Two bearded *hombres* looking like mountain men been in the hills too damn long. So we do whatever we can to gain a slight advantage.' It was Garrison's turn to smile. 'If we had suits we could ride in like a couple of Bible punchers. With a wagon, we could stand on the back and sell snake oil to the gullible.'

They ate their fill, washed down the grease with cups of hot coffee. Dublin scoured the hot pots and pans with dry sand. Garrison saddled both horses, and while Dublin packed away the cooking implements he dug deep in his saddle-bag and found his knife.

He turned, grinning as he brandishing the glittering blade. Dublin had finished packing, moved to the chaparral ridge and was gazing towards the river.

'You're first for the knife,' Garrison called.

'I don't think so.'

'Hell, just pretend I'm the Sureño barber.'

'No. We made a bad mistake.' Dublin swung on him. His face was grim beneath the beard. 'When he'd finished shooting last night, Lloyd went home. But not before he'd hung around. He must have followed us close enough to work out where we were heading. There's four of them out there, Jack. A quarter mile away. Spreading out across the slope, working their way up.'

'Young Lloyd and who else? His pa?'

'His pa was near seventy when you went in Yuma. That makes him ninety now, and none of us is young. Geraint Lloyd's pushing fifty. The other three out there … at this distance I can't tell.'

'Old train robbers?' Garrison suggested.

'Has to be.'

'Whoever it is,' Garrison said, 'if they're coming up the hill then we climb higher and faster. Live to fight another day.'

'Gets steeper. The horses will struggle. With our backs to those fellers, they'll pick us off like flies.'

'If they want us dead.'

'If they *are* those old train robbers, as long as we're alive we're a threat to their way of life.'

Garrison nodded. 'You're right. We stay here. Face them. This gully's a fortress.'

'A fortress or a trap. All I see is whichever way we look there's no way out for us if they get too close.' Dublin again moved to the edge, cautiously peered over. 'They're closing in now, Jack, and the two outside men have peeled off.'

'Looking to outflank us.'

Garrison was at the horses. He drew two Winchesters from leather, tossed one to Dublin.

'You know what they say?'

'Best form of defence is attack,' Dublin muttered. He dropped to one knee close to the tangled mesquite, slammed a shell into the Winchester's breech and opened fire.

Garrison heard faint shouts. Then he too was at what he considered the gully's ramparts. They were on south-facing foothills. The sun was high and dazzling. The attackers had it at their backs. Two men were still working their way up the slope. They were riding tough cow ponies, cutting horses accustomed to fast manoeuvring. Dublin's fire had done nothing more than alert the men. They were returning fire, snapping random shots without bothering much about aim. Nevertheless the bullets were coming close, humming like angry hornets before ricocheting off the rocks with howls like souls in torment.

'Keeping our heads down while their pards work their way round,' Garrison opined, then did the opposite. Taking a position several yards away from Dublin, he stuck his head out and began blasting away with the Winchester.

He fired fast, but with accuracy. Carefully noting the dust his shots kicked up, he adjusted his aim. Two more shots, and he brought down one of the horses. It dropped hard, slid kicking on the coarse grass. There was a wild yell as the rider tumbled. He fell awkwardly, slamming into a boulder. Garrison heard the faint but sickening snap of breaking bone. The man screamed, doubled up and grabbed his leg.

The second man saw what had happened. Now he began to place his shots with care. Dirt kicked up from the ramparts. Then Dublin uttered a strangled grunt. He dropped the rifle and fell away from the chaparral ridge. He lay awkwardly, blood bubbling from his open mouth.

With a sudden crunch and rattle of loose stone, one of the flanking riders dropped down from the rock overhang and launched himself at Garrison. The man slammed into his back as he tried to turn, sent him crashing over the ridge into the choked chaparral. As he fell, twisting at the waist, Garrison saw the fourth man come pounding into the open end of the gully. He ran at Dublin, took one glance, then lifted his six-gun and planted a bullet in the dying man's head.

Garrison roared his anger. Then the big man who had dropped from the overhang was on him again. Garrison caught the bright flash of metal in the sunlight as a powerful arm was raised. He threw himself to one side. The down-swinging pistol cracked into his shoulder. Pain deadened his arm. He groaned, kicked out fiercely, snapped his boot into his attacker's knee. The man swore. He tumbled sideways as his leg buckled. The pistol fell from his hand. He scrabbled for it, missed. Tried again and grinned savagely as his fingers closed around the butt.

His assailant was squinting at his pistol's muzzle. It was clogged with dirt. He was banging the side of the barrel against his gloved hand, desperately trying to clear the blockage.

Garrison could hear the fierce snorting of the horse further down the slope. The man with the broken leg was out of it, but the remaining man was closing in fast. And then the man who had put a bullet in Joe Dublin threatened to end the resistance. Bright sunlight threw his shadow tall against the gully's rock wall. He looked over the ridge at Garrison, levelled his pistol and cocked it with an oily click.

Garrison was down in the chaparral. The sharp thorns were stabbing his flesh, snagging his clothing. Dublin's killer was up above, grinning at him over his six-gun. The other man had succeeded in clearing the earth blockage, had cocked the gun, and was pointing it at Garrison

In the hot, still air, there was the sound of three men breathing harshly. Insects hummed their lazy way above the undergrowth. Scrub crackled as the third man worked his cow pony up the slope.

'Either one of you going to shoot?' Garrison said.

The gaunt face of the man he'd kicked in the knee was tight with pain. He ignored the question, pushed himself to his feet and waggled the pistol.

'Get back up there,' he said. 'Faster you do that, faster we're out of here.'

The man up in the gully was laughing. 'Shooting's the easy way out, and it's not for you. Yours is the hard way: you go back inside, spend the rest of your life in a cell.'

He had an educated voice. It rang with authority. Garrison had him pegged as the leader of the group. But he was well into his fifties; twenty years ago he could have been one of four men robbing a train. But again, Garrison knew he was getting ahead of himself. All he knew for sure was that the two men holding him at gunpoint were not going to shoot. That told him the third man would also have been told to take Garrison alive.

And one on one was better odds than one against two.

With a convulsive jerk Garrison freed himself from the tangle of chaparral and rolled down the slope into clear bright sunlight. He tucked his feet under him and used momentum to bring himself upright. He straightened, turned to run, and slammed into the lathered, heaving side of the snorting cow pony. The rider emitted a startled 'Hey!', then freed a foot from a stirrup and kicked at Garrison. But the spooked pony was backing away and

54

the man's foot flailed at empty air. He was off balance, twisted in the saddle with just one foot in a stirrup and his weight all wrong. He grabbed for his mount's long mane, hung on. That further disturbed the pony. It began to buck.

Garrison's break for freedom had taken the two men in the gully by surprise. But now, behind him, he could hear curses and the crackling of brush. The distance was too short. They'd be on him in seconds.

He needed a horse, and fast.

The pony was still bucking, but it was over its fright and settling. The rider had recovered his seat. He had the reins, and his free foot was searching for the stirrup. It never got there. Garrison lunged at horse and rider. He grabbed the man's belt, reached up to grasp a handful of leather vest at the neck and dragged him bodily out of the saddle. He hit the ground on his back and lay there winded. His foot was caught in the stirrup. Again the pony took fright. It reared and began to back away, but it was fighting against the man's weight and Garrison had grasped the reins and was holding them taut.

He kicked at the man's foot, trying to free the stirrup. It was twisted. Breath hissing through his teeth, the man made a grab for Garrison's leg, caught his pants. Garrison turned, kicked him in the face. There was a crunch. Blood spurted from his nose. His hand fell away.

The two men with six-guns burst out of the chaparral.

With one frenzied leap, Garrison was over the bloodied man and in the pony's saddle. Again he kicked at the stirrup, desperately trying to free the man's trapped foot, but the frightened pony was already reacting to the stranger on its back. Ears flattened, it spun with cutting-horse agility and set off down the slope.

Yelling mightily, the man with his foot in the stirrup was dragged and bounced across coarse grass, scrub, and rocks. But his luck was in. The gradient was steep, the pony forced to slow down and pick its way. Despite the warning that for him death was the easy way out and he was on his way back to the state pen, Garrison was expecting a bullet in the back. He flattened himself in the saddle. His face in the pony's mane. He held his breath. Closed his eyes.

Heard the crack of the anticipated shot.

The bullet smacked into living flesh with a dull thump. Garrison cringed, waiting for the searing agony of the bloody wound. Then his eyes snapped open. He was not the target. The pony that was his only way out of a tight spot snorted, stumbled, and went down. As the forelegs collapsed under him, Garrison was thrown over the dying pony's head. He broke his fall with both arms, bounced of the dry, hard ground. When he came down, spread-eagled, the back of his head hit a half-buried rock. The bright sun flickered and faded. In a sky that was suddenly dark, he saw stars. Gasping, he tried to move, felt the weakness in his limbs. He could hear voices, but they were disembodied, echoing inside his head.

Then he heard the always recognizable snap of a weapon being cocked.

When he opened his eyes, in the blurred, shimmering sunlight, the first thing he saw was the pony's bulk. There was no sign of life. Ironically, it had collapsed and died with its head resting on the horse Garrison had shot.

And up against the rocks, the man with the broken leg was pointing a six-gun at Garrison's head.

He looked mad enough to use it.

SEVEN

Sureño was so busy when they rode in that the four men and their prisoner dragging their personal drift of dust down the centre of main street went almost unnoticed. If anything attracted attention it was the man with the broken leg. The limb had been crudely splinted on the hillside with a branch and rawhide bindings, but he was forced to ride with that leg sticking out awkwardly, and his face was pale and bathed in sweat.

The man with the broken nose was dribbling blood; in the dazzling sunlight it looked as if his whiskers were a resplendent red. He was riding double with the man whose knee Garrison had kicked. The extent of that damage would not become obvious until he dismounted.

Before they rode down from the foothills, Joe Dublin's body had been dragged to the back of the gully under the rock overhang and covered with loose shale. The four men had lost two cutting-horses, one shot deliberately to foil Garrison's desperate break for freedom. They'd replaced one with what had become Dublin's chestnut mare. Garrison was riding his blood bay into town, but doubted if he'd ever see it again. But, hell, he thought, easy come, easy go, and losing a horse he had stolen was the least of his worries.

Once in town the men surrounding him weaved their way through wagons, riders, shoppers, and businessmen, ignoring the occasional shouted question, their aim the west end of the street and square and the sandstone building with barred windows that was, to Garrison, like a second home. It was a long time ago, but he had spent several years in there as ruler of his own small roost. Such memories never fade. And now....

Now it was Rick Garrison sitting behind the desk, about the same age as Jack had been all those years ago, and probably wearing the same tin badge. And if there was one thing that had been causing Jack Garrison intense trepidation, it was not the fear of more years of solitary confinement in Yuma but the unnerving prospect of coming face to face with his brother.

Rick Garrison had grown from child to manhood while brother Jack was suffering in a hard stone cell where the sunlight painted across the dirt floor was always striped. Had he matured in the Garrison mould – whatever that might be – and if so would that be good or bad for both their futures? Would he now look at his older brother with all the compassion, the horror, the sadness that had been in his eyes and his pale face when he was five years old? Or would he take one look at the ragged, bearded escaped prisoner, turn away with obvious contempt, and have a deputy throw him in a cell?

Garrison would soon know.

They'd allowed him his banjo. It knocked against his back when he was ordered to dismount at the hitch rail fronting the jail. The jolt as he slid from the saddle and his heels hit the ground sent pain knifing through his skull; the fall against the rock down from the gully had caused minor concussion. The steps onto the plank walk rocked under him the way a canoe rocks under a careless man who stands in mid-stream. A hard hand in the small of the back propelled him ahead of the man he'd pegged as leader. He stumbled once. Then he was through the open door, and the cool air contained by the jail's stone walls touched the sweat on his face with icy chill.

'Brought someone to see you, Rick,' the leader said, tossing Garrison's gunbelt onto the desk.

A tall man uncoiled from a swivel chair. He was lean and hungry-looking, bony but wide of shoulder, stern of countenance but with laugh lines crinkling the corners of his eyes. He had that certain cat-like poise which meant, in Jack Garrison's experience, a man relaxed to the point of indolence but ready to spring into action at the first sign of danger.

In that instant of recognition of a type, Jack Garrison was twenty years younger and looking in what his ma had called a cheval mirror.

'Goddammit,' he said huskily, 'you've not seen me in twenty years yet you managed to grow in my image.'

But Marshal Rick Garrison was not looking at him. His eyes were on the big man who'd escorted Jack into the jail.

'I wondered where you'd got to, Raker. I got back from Yuma to find young Lynch struggling to hold the fort while coming down with a fever.' He jerked a thumb. 'And how and where did you find him?'

'He rode into town, asked after you, then a while after that had a set to with Joe Dublin in Mackie's. Lynch was there, him and Corcoran sorted it out. After that …' Raker shrugged. 'He didn't know it, but someone thought they recognized him and got word to me. I had a walk around, but he'd left town. Then Joe Dublin rode out, pushing that tired old paint he rides. I called in some help, we rode out about midnight, and early this morning we got Garrison and Dublin boxed in up in the Eagle tail foothills. Bullets started flying. Dublin's dead. Ellis's leg's broke, Lloyd has a sore knee—'

'Geraint Lloyd?'

'Yeah, he wanted in on it.'

'He's old, in his fifties, for Christ's sake.'

'And now he's old and in pain,' Raker said. He shrugged his shoulders. 'Soames, he was drug by his horse and ain't feeling too good. We lost two horses but—'

There was something in his voice that alerted Jack Garrison. When the big man, Raker, pushed him to one side and moved closer to the desk, sunlight slanting through the window caught the glint of tin. Jack noticed, for the first time, that he was wearing a badge. Well, his brother's earlier questioning of the man had made that clear, but what intrigued Jack was that Raker had not been ordered by the marshal to bring in the escaped convict.

61

Again, that had been made clear by Raker: the manhunt had been done on the deputy's initiative. To ensure success he had ridden out with three armed men. He'd named those three, but who were they? The man called Ellis had a broken leg, Lloyd was suffering from Jack Garrison's vicious kick, and Soames had been dragged down the hillside with sharp rocks raking his back. All three had a clear excuse to drift away in search of a doc to tend to their wounds. Highly convenient, in Jack Garrison's opinion, and it gave him food for thought.

'You did well, Raker.'

His brother was nodding, his face thoughtful as he looked somewhat absently past Jack to the open door. 'Now finish it off. Take him out back to a cell, lock him up – and if you lose the key, that's fine by me.'

Without another word, without the slightest acknowledgement that the bearded ruffian Raker had brought in from the hills was his brother, Marshal Rick Garrison strode out of the jail.

For Jack Garrison, that day dragged. He had been locked up midway through the morning. He spent most of the long hours after the cell door clanged shut smoking, dozing, and idly watching the pattern of bars moving across the dirt floor. It was about as interesting as watching grass grow, which would take what seemed like eternity in some parts of Arizona. Though he was aware of the familiar noises of a working town – voices, shouts, the whinnying of horses, the rumble of wagon wheels – he saw nobody and was left entirely alone until the onset of dusk. Then, startling him out of increasing lethargy, the door leading to the office banged open and in the evening gloom Deputy Raker came through carrying a tray of food and drink.

The conveying of that late meal to Garrison involved a complicated procedure involving tray, keys, and the tricky juggling of a six-gun once the cell door was open. Not a word was spoken. The tray was placed carelessly on the dirt floor, spilling already cold coffee, the cell door was locked, and that was that.

Of Marshal Rick Garrison, there was still no sign.

The meat was cold and tough, the hunk of bread grey with mould, the coffee cold and bitter. In a sudden burst of anger Garrison spat out the first half-chewed mouthful, and kicked out violently. The tray, tin plate, and cup flew through the air to clang against the strap steel bars and clatter to the floor.

Shaking with anger, Garrison flopped onto the hard cot. Lit a cigarette. Then, with as little conscious thought as a man gives to his breathing, he reached out for his banjo and began to pick some of his favourite tunes. His pulse slowed, returned to normal. He leaned back, closed his eyes, lost himself in the music.

At some time in the next hour he must have fallen asleep. An indeterminate time after that he came awake, stiff, cold, smelling singed blanket that told him he'd dropped his cigarette as he slept, and with the knowledge that he had been woken by the rattle of keys.

The cell door was open.

His brother was standing over him.

'Get up, Jack,' Rick Garrison said. 'If we're going to get you out of here, we have to move fast.'

PART TWO

EIGHT

'Where's Raker?'

'It's his night off. We take turns. Should be Lynch, but he's sick.'

'Tonight's way different. Raker locked up your brother—'

'I gave the order.'

'But not to go after me. That was his initiative, and done out of desperation. Now common sense will warn him, set alarm bells ringing. At the very least he'll be thinking of what you might get up to, see you opening the cell so we can set talking, catch up on those missing twenty years; see you getting careless and maybe turning your back—'

'The fault in your reasoning,' Rick Garrison cut in, 'is in supposing a lowly deputy in his fifties is going to be sitting at home worrying about what might be happening in the jail. Why would he do that?'

'If you don't know now,' Jack Garrison said, 'then that's one of the subjects we'll be discussing when we get wherever it is we're going.'

'If you didn't leave most of your brains in Yuma,' Marshal Rick Garrison said, 'you'll have known we're going into hiding from the moment I opened the cell door.'

They had left the jail office openly, stepping out into bright moonlight that made any attempt at stealth impossible. An oil lamp hung over the desk from where Jack collected his gunbelt, and Rick had left that burning and the front door wide open. Deputy Raker had taken Jack's blood bay to the livery barn, which was where Rick kept his horse when in town. Crossing the deserted street to collect their mounts – again without any attempt at stealth – they were spotted by a man who came stumbling unsteadily across the pool of lamplight outside Mackie's saloon.

'Hey, Marshal,' he called, 'you know your office door's open?'

'I'm letting some air in, some flies out.'

'Yeah, tha's OK, but I hear you got a prish ... a prisoner, an' if you leave doors open—'

'Go home to your wife, feller.'

'Ain't you going to introdoosh ... duce me to your hairy friend?'

'This is my poor, grey-haired pa, come back from the dead. And if you don't want to spend the night in a cell, you'll do as I say and go home.'

Leaving the drunken man gaping at the idea of resurrection, they were across the street and in the livery barn, nodding to the hostler and walking down the runway to the stalls. Five minutes later they were mounted and riding out of town. They kept their horses to a steady walk. Then, with the warm glow of oil lamps blurring behind them in the night-time river mists, they upped the gait to a ground-covering canter and headed west along the Gila River.

After a mile, Rick wheeled his sorrel away from the river. They pushed on for another couple of miles, off-trail and riding through chaparral and greasewood, with the tall shapes of saguaro and Spanish Dagger looking uncannily like men lurking in the shadows. When they had gained the higher, drier, naked ground leading to the Mohawk foothills he wheeled left again so that they were riding back towards Sureño but to the south of the town and some way above it.

And now Jack knew the location Rick had in mind.

At some time in the past a band of Apache Indians had chosen a small box canyon as a suitable place for a village. Because of the searing heat and scarcity of rain in Arizona, the Apache's wickiups had survived remarkably well. The frameworks that had once been green saplings had hardened, become brittle, and here and there snapped to bring part of a dwelling tumbling down. But of those wickiups that had survived, many still had sagging roofs of bark and rushes that would provide anyone who camped there with shelter from the heat.

More importantly, the high rock face at the canyon's boxed end had given the Apaches security against any assault from above other than by long range rifle fire, while the canyon's downhill opening sloped away so steeply that no United States soldiers could have approached without being seen.

If the village in the canyon was to be their hideout for any length of time, Jack mused, those qualities so appreciated by the Apaches could come in useful.

They were riding across the raking slopes of the foothills. Below, fascinating Jack after his years of confinement, the oil lamps of Sureño were like fireflies flickering across the flat ground. The gentle curve of the Gila River that formed the town's northern boundary was picked out by the high, pale moon.

He shook his head, nostalgia welling.

Rick, riding a little higher up the slope, caught the direction of Jack's gaze. He brought the sorrel down, and closer. They both drew rein, lit cigarettes, sat for a few moments smoking in silence as they looked down on the town.

In the far distance a horse whinnied. Jack's roan pricked up its ears, blew through its nostrils. The sorrel turned its head, eyes shining in the moonlight. Bridle metal jingled, crisp grass crunched under shod hoofs as the horses moved restlessly, eager to push on.

The quiet was broken by Rick. Years of absence and the years between their respective ages made little difference: they were brothers, and he had followed Jack's thinking without difficulty.

'You know that when we doubled back we rode past the old house?'

'I should have. I was looking for it just now, but I guess my brain's gone dull from doing too much catching up,'

Jack said. He looked across at his brother. 'You still live there?'

'Not any more.'

'Ah.' Jack nodded, feeling a sudden surge of guilt. 'As of tonight you've got no home, no job – that right?'

'Right. I turned rogue lawman and freed a convicted train robber,' Rick said. 'That makes Deputy Raker the new town marshal, and the Garrison house is the first place he'll go looking.'

'And all this has come about because I rode into town and upset the apple-cart.'

'You couldn't be more wrong,' Rick Garrison said. 'You've been in my thoughts from the day I saw you taken away in irons.'

'You saying that's why you took the job? Following in big brother's footsteps?'

'No. I took the job of town marshal because that made me a lawman, and the law was what put you away. What do they say, always better to be inside the tent pissing out? I became part of the system, in the hope that by doing so I'd find out why you were framed. Because you were, and I know it. I've heard men talking. Not enough for me to move on, nothing definite enough for me to make arrests.'

'And here's me,' Jack said huskily, 'believing you couldn't bear to look at my face when Raker brought me in.'

Rick laughed. 'You were right. One look at your ugly face and I was so happy I'd have given the game away. Before that face-to-face we were both alone, Jack. Then you clawed your way over that prison wall, and we're together again – and together we'll find out who set you up, and make them pay dear.'

NINE

They spent the night in the nearest wickiup to the canyon's entrance, rolled in smelly, sweat-soaked saddle-blankets to ward off the chill of the mountain air. They'd gone to sleep hungry, pulling in their belts a notch because food was something they were short of and the next day's breakfast seemed a more important meal.

Dawn saw Jack up first and on his knees. He had taken a tin bowl out of the roan's saddle-bags, filled it with ice-cold water from one of the canteens, and was hacking away at his beard with the knife he had brandished at Joe Dunlop but not got around to using. His eyes were crinkled with pain, and leaking tears. Shaving by feel meant his fingers soon became tipped with blood. When Rick rolled out of his blankets, he was confronted by the gruesome sight of a brother he barely recognized.

'Don't know if it's an improvement,' Rick commented critically. 'Most men *grow* beards to hide their identity, so at least it's a new twist.'

For a while they shivered outside the wickiup that

had provided some protection from the cold of the high ground, shoulders hunched and their breath pluming white as they gazed out of the box canyon and down the long slopes covered in grass that was glistening with dew but as brown as the earth it sparsely covered. The smoke from their cigarettes mingled with the vapour of their breath. They were yet to light a fire. Other than the bowl Jack had used for shaving, the supplies and means of preparing a hot meal were still buckled inside the roan's saddle-bags.

For some reason neither of the men could yet fathom, their mood was gloomy. There was an oppressive air of foreboding. They were both thinking, reflecting on where they might have made mistakes, but it was Rick who noticed the first indication that things were indeed going badly wrong.

Far below, to the west of the town, a slim pencil of white smoke pointed towards the clear blue skies. At its base, a fire glowed red.

'You remember I said we rode past the house?' Rick said.

'The fog's gone from my brain,' Jack said. 'Doesn't take long for a man to get accustomed to freedom.'

'Well, that's it, there,' Rick said, his voice grim, and he pointed at the pencil of white smoke.

'*What*? You saying they've burned down your house, your home?'

'*Our* home. But, yes, I made a mistake. One of the reasons I chose this location was because we needed time and space to think. The house wasn't suitable; I knew that

74

was the first place Raker would go looking. What I didn't expect was for him to vent his anger and hatred.'

'Why should he hate you?'

Rick hesitated. 'A good point. There's no reason why he should, so hatred's the wrong word. I think what drove him and his cronies into our house with flaming torches was fear.'

'The fear I can understand, if Raker's involved with the men I'm after,' Jack said, his eyes still lingering in disbelief on the distant fire that was destroying memories of his childhood.

'Somewhere out there there's a man with a lot to lose,' Rick mused. 'That man's still giving orders. Maybe it's him, not you, that Raker and the others fear.'

'Or me and him, in equal measure.' He glanced at Rick. 'That man with a lot to lose. He was behind the train robbery?'

'If I'm right. And if he does exist, he's a ruthless man but a man with brains and cunning.'

'Also,' Jack said, 'continuing on your line of thought, he would be someone who needed money for some reason more important than mere lust for gold.'

'Brains, cunning, and you're saying ambition.' Rick nodded. 'I'd say all three of those attributes rule out Elgan Lloyd.'

'An ambitious man looking at crime to further his own ends,' Jack ventured, 'would stay well out of sight, then and now. He'd always pay others to do the dirty work.'

There was silence for a few beats.

'You'll remember the story of the posse out of Yuma?'

Rick said at last. 'The pursuit, three train robbers hanged from tall aspens, and the one that got away with the money?'

Jack smiled wryly. 'According to the law, that man was me. But I was a scapegoat. The only sign of stolen money was a few notes, and those government issue sacks that were used to prove my guilt.'

'Sure,' Rick said, 'but why was there a need for someone to take the rap? And there's another point that stinks to high heaven: not too long after you were locked up there was a rumour going around that the manhunt was pure fiction. There was no posse, no train robbers were ever caught and hanged. If rumour was fact, those men – and it's four ageing train robbers, not three, because you were never one of them – must still be around, settled in middle age, and being driven by fear.'

'As for me right now,' Jack said in carefully measured tones, 'it's not fear I feel but apprehension that's been growing by the minute.'

Rick smiled. 'I thought all your attention was on the fire.'

'Oh no. I've been watching them from the moment they came out of the river mist on the far side of the town trail. Three riders. Cut through the trees, taking the short way. Too far away to see clearly, but hows about I make some educated guesses? Can't be the man called Ellis, his leg was broken when I shot his horse. Soames? Well, he was dragged when I used his horse to take off in a hurry, but he looked OK, and Geraint Lloyd had nothing worse than a sore knee. That's two possibles. I'd say Raker could be the other man, but how the hell did they find us so soon?'

'I've been thinking about that feller in town,' Rick said. 'Looks like he was no drunk, and I was a fool to think we could get clean away. Someone was bound to see us, and he did: saw us come out of the jail, listened to me cracking jokes and acting tough, then went hotfoot to give someone the news.'

'We were followed. I remember now we heard a horse when we stopped to talk and smoke a cigarette,' Jack said, 'and thought nothing of it.' His gaze ranged over the landscape, the steep slopes, the river in the distance. When he looked at Rick his clean-shaven jaw was set, his eyes steely. 'Tell me, did your deputy get around to saying how he caught me and Joe Dublin?'

'The last word we exchanged was when I told him to throw you in a cell.'

Jack grinned. 'Yeah, well, Raker led an intelligent assault on what me and Joe figured was as safe a location as we could get: a gully a ways up the Eagle Tail foothills. The four of them came at us head on, then a man rode out wide on each flank. Before we knew it they were on us, one dropping down over the high cliff, the other coming in from the side. We were as good as dead. I made a break, almost got away.' He shrugged. 'I was rusty from too much time served, but what happened on that hillside taught me a hard lesson. This situation's similar; a gully then, a box canyon now. Yesterday we were caught cold. It won't happen again.'

*

They'd stabled the two horses inside one of the larger wickiups. It was the work of just few minutes to get them out and saddled. They'd had nothing but rough grazing, but seemed happy enough when Rick splashed water from the remaining canteen into his hat and gave them drinks. Jack was first in the saddle. He rode to the canyon entrance, knowing that he would be spotted at once but that the game was up anyway.

The three men were now less than a mile away. The early morning sunlight flashed on bright metal: all three riders were carrying rifles. A hand was raised as one of the men shouted something, and pointed.

'That's that, then,' Rick said, spotting the man's excited gesture as he brought his sorrel alongside Jack's roan. 'I thought we might have snuck away unseen, but we've left it too late.'

'Three on two,' Jack said reflectively. 'That's not bad odds.'

'I thought you'd ruled out fighting in a tight corner? It won't happen again, isn't that what you said?'

'What I meant was no tricky sonofabitch is going to outsmart me. Weighing up the situation, I'd say all that open terrain and the layout of the canyon leaves them no option. They'll come at us from the front. There's no other way. We've got the high ground and can find cover. That gives us the edge.'

'Maybe so,' Rick said, 'but I didn't walk you out of jail so you could take a bullet in the head. If it comes down to a gunfight, one of us could end up dead….'

'They're pushing their horses hard, closing in fast.

We're running out of time.'

'And wasting it talking.'

Even as he mouthed the words, in a sudden burst of impatience, Rick was spurring his horse out of the canyon's mouth. It took Jack an instant to react. Then he raked the roan lightly with his spurs' blunted rowels and was out of the canyon. The horse sprang eagerly into a canter, then stretched out in a full-blown gallop. It caught up with the sorrel in a dozen ground-eating strides. Together the brothers raced across the hillside, brushing through chaparral, their horses' metal hoofs ringing and drawing flinty sparks from treacherous rock slabs, their hat brims flattened by the wind.

Half a mile below, the three men drew rein. They turned their horses side on, settled in the saddles, and opened fire. Rifle muzzles flashed red. Gunsmoke rose like a dark pall in the still, clear air.

'Dammit, they're going for the horses,' Jack yelled.

As bullets began kicking up chunks of earth, he saw Rick nod understanding. Then, knowing his brother would understand and follow, Jack leaned back in the saddle and wrenched the roan around in a tight turn. Again using the blunt spurs, he urged the big roan down the slope.

'Straight at them,' he cried over his shoulder. 'They want trouble, we'll give it to 'em.'

Head on, they'd have made difficult targets even if they'd ridden straight. They didn't. Using knees and reins they caused the two horses to jink left and right, again and again. Rifle bullets buzzed like angry hornets, but always cut harmlessly through thin air. The gunmen were too slow to react to the horses' swerving runs. Always fractions of a second late adjusting their aim, the firing ceased abruptly as they began to panic. The two big horses were bearing down on them like rogue outlaw broncs. Jack and Rick were flattened along their necks, adding to the impression that they were wild, riderless horses out of control.

Frantic yells ripped the air apart. Brush crackled under flashing hoofs. There was a quick wheeling of mounts, a hauling on taut reins, a desperate attempt to clear a path. But their horses were rolling their eyes, the whites showing as they snorted and milled and got even more tangled.

Then Jack and Rick were on them, and the tangle turned into crunching, bone-shaking contact.

They battered their way through. The big roan hit a smaller horse with a shoulder. Its weight knocked the animal sideways, unseating the rider. He threw his hands in the air and went down with a strangled yell. His rifle flew high, glittering in the sunlight. Rick's sorrel smacked into a second horse. Again the rider went down, hitting the ground and curling as he went under the hoofs of his panicked mount. The third man got clear. His horse was ready to bolt but he strained to hold it back. He'd dropped his rifle, but twisted in the saddle and got off three snapped shots with his six-gun. But again his bullets cut through empty space. Then his horse reared. The rider went backwards out of the saddle, hit the ground hard and lay still.

Geraint Lloyd. A sore head to add to his aching knee. Jack grinned in triumph. The way was clear. They were through.

Behind them as they rode down the levelling slope and hit fertile grassland, someone yelled. A shot was fired. The bullet plucked at Jack's shirt, burning his skin, and he knew they'd been lucky and that it couldn't last. But another half mile saw them through the trees and onto the river trail. Out of sight. Nothing stopping them from riding on – but riding where? Out of Sureño? Out of Arizona? Jack knew the temptation would be there, for both of them. But he also knew that it would never work because a clean break would leave too much unfinished.

Breathless, he said, 'You recognize anybody?'

'Nobody on either side was studying faces, but I'm pretty sure Deputy Raker wasn't there.'

'Then we need to take care. The last thing we want is one of us back in jail. I say we split up.'

'I agree. Get together again later, somewhere—'

'Last night I met Joe at the creek,' Jack said. 'You know the one I mean?'

'Poco a Poco? Dry as a bone yard, everybody knows it.'

'And I'm not superstitious. Being there didn't do Joe a lot of good in the end, but it still seems a good place to meet. They won't be expecting me to use it twice.'

'That's tonight, under cover of darkness. Leaves a lot of time to kill.'

'Then, in our own way, we make those hours count. Together we've been acting like fools.'

'I'm the fool. It was me led the way.'

'And I followed, so I'm as much to blame. You got me out of jail, Rick, don't forget that, but messing around in Indian wickiups was playing schoolboy games. Camping out under the stars. Smoking a first cigarette. Is that the best we can do? Hell, I really don't understand what we thought we were playing at, but that kind of stupidity has to end.'

'You taking over?'

'Well, it's only right it should come back to me, to end up as my responsibility. And although I've been away for an extended vacation' – he flashed a grin – 'I can see that hasn't put me out of touch. In a small town like Sureño nothing changes from one year to the next. Elgan Lloyd, for instance. He's old, now, but still in his old house. According to Joe Dublin, he's got his son living there with him.'

He couldn't keep the sudden excitement out of his voice at the realization that Joe Dublin had pointed the way and there was something he could do to take the fight to the enemy. Rick was on to it in a flash.

'Stay away from Elgan Lloyd.'

'Well now. I obeyed orders for twenty years. I appreciate your concern, Rick, but it's about time I got used to making my own decisions. I had a dust up with Lloyd a couple of years before my sojourn in Yuma. He was so angry the spittle was flying, so you can bet your boots he'll be pleased to see me again. Asking that man some hard questions should make for an interesting day.'

TEN

In Sureño there was a greasy café that was a little way off the main street, tucked in the middle of a block of vacant premises gathering dust from lack of use. It was a quiet backwater in the small Arizona river town, and that suited Jack Garrison. He'd eaten yesterday's breakfast up the Eagle Tail foothills, angrily kicked last night's supper against the bars in what had been his brother's jail, and the morning's breakfast was still buckled in his saddle-bags.

Rick had gone his own way, saying nothing. There was a considerable risk in Jack's riding through town, and sight of the jail's barred windows gave him an uncomfortable few moments. But although the door was open – hell, had it been that way since they'd walked out last night? – there was no sign of life inside the office. Once he was past, the danger was over. The bustle of activity on the main street reduced him to being just one more rider on a range-dusty horse, and the last time he'd been moving freely in town he'd been a bearded old man with a banjo.

The banjo might have been a giveaway. He clung to it the way a little girl might cling to a favourite doll – and that amused him for a moment when he thought of the way he'd sounded off at Rick. But, banjo or not, he made it to the café without incident.

Fifteen minutes later he had greasy fingers, a satisfyingly full belly, and was standing at the café's hitch rail feeding the roan handfuls of oats provided by the proprietor. In that position he had his back to the Gila River that flowed half a mile away behind the café. On the banks of the river, some fifteen miles away in a westerly direction, lay Tredegar, the spread established by Elgan Lloyd's Welsh grandparents.

If he was serious about asking the 90-year-old some awkward questions, it was time to ride.

In the days before his incarceration, Jack Garrison had always been a reckless youngster with a devil-may-care outlook on life. Risks were there to be taken, and though he followed that creed too often for his own good, he had never been a fool.

He was well aware that the ride west to the Lloyd spread would take him perilously close to the Mohawk foothills, and it was quite likely that the three men he and Rick had so violently brushed aside would be making their painful way down the slopes. With that danger in mind, he rode along the main street, cut down the alley opposite the jail, and made his way down to the river.

The banks were, at first, steep grass slopes. Close to the river they flattened out and became narrow expanses of coarse shingle that stretched for miles along the river's course. Jack Garrison rode along those. With his horse at a steady trot, its hoofs crunched pleasantly. Jack knew that the high river-banks hid him from view and, as the roan ate up the miles towards the Lloyd spread, he had time to think.

His thoughts were mostly on what he would say to old man Lloyd, but he was also marvelling at the way his escape from Yuma had opened a can of worms. When taken by Raker and his cronies in the fierce fighting in the Eagle Tail foothills, he had been told bluntly that he would spend the rest of his life behind bars. Fair enough. A deputy had led an armed posse to hunt down an escaped prisoner, and he had been recaptured.

But there had been a ferocious intensity in the posse's demeanour, a hint of desperation in their desire to see him back in prison. As for today's incident on the slopes of the Mohawks, it was obvious that the three men were now not concerned with recapturing him. They had drawn rein and sprayed the hillside with deadly rifle fire – and while Rick had said the men were trying to bring down the horses, Jack had his doubts.

They wanted him dead; dead men don't talk.

So what did that tell him?

Whoever was desperate to silence him must know he was no train robber. By proving his innocence, he would inevitably expose those who had laid a clever smokescreen that for years had covered their own guilt. That was unlikely to be of concern to a gang of armed bandits who had robbed a train twenty years ago. Besides, the rumour that they had been hanged by the neck in a grove of tall aspens meant that they had never been in danger of detection.

Until now.

As a marshal, Jack had jailed young Geraint Lloyd for rustling and brought Elgan Lloyd's wrath down on his head. The father had vowed to make Garrison pay, but it was insane to believe he had staged the train robbery for that purpose. What was much more likely was that Lloyd had already been involved in a complicated plot, and had seized the opportunity to frame Jack Garrison.

Lloyd had always been a landowner, and rarely short of cash. So why had he become involved in crime? Why would he risk everything to make another man rich? That suggested the brains behind the train robbery had some kind of hold over Lloyd. Fair enough. Lloyd had followed orders, arranged for men in his employ to do the dirty work, and the big man pocketed the proceeds.

But the violence rained down on Jack to silence him told another clear tale: twenty years of comfortable living still left the unknown man vulnerable. He was running scared.

Jack Garrison's hope was that old man Lloyd could give him that man's name.

ELEVEN

The way it worked out, the old man came to Jack a while before he reached Lloyd's spread.

The Tredegar ranch house was a good half-mile away from the Gila, but the family had always been protective of their water rights in a territory dominated by the year-round scorching sun. So the Lloyd fences – now so badly neglected they were mostly rotting timber and rusty wire – came all the way down to the river. It was when he reached the first of these that Jack brought the blood roan up off the wet gravel and onto the higher ground.

From that first vantage point, avoiding discovery by staying well back from the tree-lined crest of a low rise, he saw a buckboard stopped beneath the unpainted timber uprights and heavy cross beam marking the entrance to Tredegar. The far side of the trail that stretched from Sureño in the general direction of Yuma was cloaked in more thick stands of trees. That dark background acted as camouflage, reducing men in dark clothing to indistinct figures against the patterns of branches and leaves.

Nevertheless, Jack could see that two men were on board the wagon. The driver was waiting to move off. Jack hadn't seen old man Lloyd for twenty years, but the buckboard's passenger wore a black suit and black hat, there was the glint of a gold watch chain across his vest and he looked bent and frail.

There were two riders alongside the buckboard. Lloyd was talking to one of them. The rider was leaning far out of the saddle to catch the spoken words. Even at a distance that man was recognizable. Jack had seen him twice recently, both times at close quarters. The first time he'd been on his back in chaparral, staring straight into the yawning muzzle of the man's six-gun; only hours ago he had knocked him off his horse, gazed down at the stunned man's pale face.

It was Geraint Lloyd. No doubt he had told his father of the botched encounter on the high slopes that meant Jack Garrison was still on the loose. He seemed to listen to the old man a while longer, nodded, then pulled away. Both riders backed off. They watched as the buckboard driver cracked his whip, drove the short distance from the gates to the trail, and turned towards town.

The banjo strapped across Jack's back would be a hindrance in the event of lively action. He took it off, and strapped it behind the saddle. Then he moved the roan up closer to the trees, keeping them between him and the approaching buckboard.

The difficulties he had anticipated in getting into Tredegar had been solved. Lloyd had as good as walked into his arms. As the buckboard drew level and went past,

Lloyd and the driver were looking away from Jack. Their heads were dipped, hat brims shielding their eyes from the dazzling sun. All to the good. Knowing Jack Garrison was on the loose, they'd be expecting trouble. The driver would have a shotgun, Lloyd maybe a hideaway derringer. But the noise of the buckboard as it rattled along the rutted trail would mask all other sounds. The time to hit them was now.

But what about Geraint Lloyd and his companion? A searching glance back towards the drive into Tredegar told Jack that the two riders were still lingering; still talking as they idly watched the receding buckboard. Then, as one, they wheeled their mounts and headed up the long drive towards the house.

Jack waited thirty seconds to make sure they had dismissed the buckboard from their minds and were going about their business. Then he took the roan crashing straight through the scrub under the trees. He came out on the trail fifty yards behind the buckboard, and swiftly closed the distance. He was riding through the dust cloud thrown up by the wagon's metal-rimmed wheels, which were rattling, crunching on stones. The wagon's boards were creaking and groaning, the frisky horse in the traces kicking up its own share of noise.

But the driver was a young man, with sharp ears, specially chosen for the job. He heard Jack coming when he was still yards away, yelled at old man Lloyd, and stood up with legs braced wide and lashed the horse into a fast run.

Behind them the roan was already at full gallop,

almost up with the buckboard. Jack saw Lloyd turning in his seat, the black suit like a dull shadow in the sunlight, the wink of bright metal as the old man fell sideways in his efforts to tug out the hideaway pistol.

Gritting his teeth, Jack took the roan right up against the wagon's tailboard and leaped out of the saddle. He landed on his feet, clutching at the side rails. The big horse wheeled away, head high, reins and stirrups flapping. The wild rocking motion of the buckboard threw Jack flat. He hit the boards, came off them in a bound and threw himself at the old man. He rapped an arm around thin, bony shoulders. His right hand whipped his six-gun out of his holster. With a short, chopping motion he knocked the derringer out of the old man's hand, splitting the papery skin. He let his restraining arm slip up from bony chest to scrawny throat, and yelled at the driver.

'Slow down, then pull over onto the grass and stop the wagon. Do it now, or I'll break Lloyd's neck.'

The wagon was rocking, bouncing, hurtling along the trail. The young driver twisted to look over his shoulder. His gaze took in the situation. His lips tightened. He was probably under orders: if Jack Garrison gets close, ride like hell, stop for nothing. That put him in a fix. Garrison wasn't close; he was on the buckboard and choking the old man.

He kept the wagon going for another twenty, thirty, forty yards. Then, as Jack simply waited him out, he sat down with a thump and hauled on the traces. The lathered horse slowed, trotted, walked. The driver guided it onto the grass, applied the buckboard's brake.

'Let the brake off and take it in further,' Jack said. 'I want it up against the trees, out of the sun.' With that done and the wagon again at a halt, he said, 'Now unbuckle your gunbelt. If you've got a shotgun, leave it where it is under the seat. Throw down the whip. Get down, walk through those trees a way, and relax. Light a cigarette. Enjoy the view over the river. When I've finished with Lloyd, I'll give you a shout.'

'You've finished now,' Lloyd said, his voice like a fingernail scraping dry velum.

The young driver looked at Lloyd, saw nothing to help him and with gloved fingers fiddled with his heavy belt buckle. The gunbelt and six-gun clattered to the seat. He sneered at Jack, jumped down, and walked away towards the river.

Jack watched him for a moment, then released Lloyd and stepped over the seat back. He took the driver's place, cocked his six-gun and held it loosely in his lap. Then he took his first good look at Elgan Lloyd.

Ninety, Joe Dublin had said, which was about right. So he was old, scrawny, and breathing in short rasps that wracked his body. From the way he had spoken Jack had expected to see strength, if not of body then of spirit. But if anything, those words had not been for Jack, but for the old man himself: a way of reminding himself that he must keep his mouth shut. A man's eyes will always give him away. The thin old man in the black suit who was nursing his bleeding hand was staring fixedly at Jack Garrison, not just with hatred, although there was enough of that. What surprised Jack was that the hatred was overshadowed by fear.

Few frail men in their nineties fear death.

Elgan Lloyd was white-lipped with fear.

'All right,' Jack said softly, 'let's get down to it. I don't know how long we've got, so you're going to talk fast. You're going to tell me exactly why one ordinary middle-aged convict breaking out of jail after twenty years has got half of Arizona territory up in arms.'

TWELVE

Phoenix, Arizona

'You made a mistake, and it's coming back to haunt you.'

'I don't make mistakes now, and I didn't make a mistake then. I've told you many times, I was never directly involved.'

'That's exactly what I mean. That was your mistake. You should have been involved. You had a hold over Elgan Lloyd, but you stood back and gave him a free hand. You left important decisions affecting our lives to a small-town councillor who spent his spare time milking cows.'

Ella Rome was furious. Beneath the greying hair her face was flushed. She was sitting stiffly in a tall, straight-backed chair at one end of a long, mahogany dining table. Ornate suspended brass oil lamps cast warm light on her dress and touched glittering highlights in the string of pearls at her throat, on silverware, fine bone china, on crystal wine glasses, and the decanter of red wine that was almost empty.

Her husband was sitting in the chair at the other end of the table. The senator for Arizona, Jefferson T. Rome, was leaning back, but he was far from relaxed. He had a serviette tucked into the open neck of his white shirt; they had not long finished dinner. Rome's white hair, always worn rakishly long at the neck, was untidy. When he dabbed at his pale, perspiring face with a mono-grammed handkerchief, there was a noticeable tremor in his fingers.

'Lloyd did as well as we could have expected,' Rome said. 'The train was robbed, the money was spirited away.' He managed a faint smile, because they both knew what that meant. 'Within twenty-four hours, a posse hanged three men.'

'That was rumour. The train robbers are alive.'

'Of course they're alive, and I've been paying each and every one of them for years. That was the deal we cut, and my word is my bond.'

Ignoring the sharp look, the undignified snort of con-tempt, he went on, 'When the posse came out of Yuma, three convicted killers rode with them, men already under sentence of death. They were hanged in those aspen swamps. Later, the Sureño marshal spread the word that the train robbers had paid the penalty.'

'Really?' Ella was shaking her head. 'That wasn't very clever, was it? Guards died in that hold-up, but those that lived told their story and it was common knowledge that four men stopped the train. If four convicted men had been hanged, you wouldn't be staring at financial and

94

political ruin. The simple way is always the best. Instead, it seems you went for complications and decided a scapegoat was needed.'

'For God's sake!' Rome slammed both palms on the table, threatening to shatter wine glasses. 'The hanging alone would never have worked, because people either didn't believe the story, or were just plain uninterested. My hands had to be seen to be lily white – remember that? – and to make certain we needed a show trial and conviction. When Jack Garrison was sent to Yuma for life, people saw a train robber getting his comeuppance. But it went further than that. Villains always have a certain glamour attached to them. Garrison became a figure of myth and legend, a local hero, because he thumbed his nose at authority and went to prison without ever revealing where he'd hidden the stolen money.'

'Which he couldn't of course, because he was innocent,' Ella said, smiling sweetly. 'But now he's out of prison, justifiably intent on revenge, and you're in deep trouble.'

'Oh no, it's a long way from that.' Rome shook his head. 'The warden informed me by telegraph when Garrison went over the wall. This morning a rider came here from Sureño. Garrison's brother walked out of the marshal's job. His deputy's taken over, so there's now a Lloyd man in office. And you can bet Lloyd is doing everything he can to save his own hide. He saves his hide, he saves mine, and your jewellery and fine clothes are safe.'

'Would you put that in plain English?'

'I'm reasonably certain,' Jefferson Rome said, 'that the escaped convict, Jack Garrison, will already have been apprehended, and shot to death while resisting arrest.'

And now Ella's smile was enigmatic, a fact that didn't escape Rome and presented him with another worry.

'You'd better hope you're right, my dear,' she said, getting up to leave the table. 'If Jack Garrison gets into a position where he can put pressure on Lloyd, you can be damn sure the old man will spill the beans. If that happens, Garrison will come after you.'

'Ah yes, he will if he gets the chance,' Rome said to her insolent, departing back. 'But what you're not taking into account is that I have a secret weapon.'

THIRTEEN

'A man serving a life sentence for robbery and murder has escaped from the penitentiary. He must be recaptured very quickly before he kills again. The unusual activity in and around Sureño should not surprise you.'

Elgan Lloyd spoke the words without emotion. He had knotted a 'kerchief around his bloody hand. The derringer lay between his shiny ankle boots. Close, but an awkward place to reach for an old man with stiffening joints.

'You sound like the prison warden, up on a soap box addressing his officers,' Jack said. 'Trouble is, the order seems to have gone out that it's kill, not recapture. Someone, somewhere, is getting desperate.'

'That man should be you. If you had any sense you'd be enjoying endless lazy days getting rid of that jail pallor on a sunny beach in Mexico. Instead, you're here in Sureño pursuing a lost cause. You cannot win. You're a dead man walking, Garrison.'

'And I wonder who it will be breathes a sigh of relief

when I'm dead? You see, it had to be you planned that train hold-up. Your men chopped down trees and stopped the train, got away with a fortune in bank notes. But according to Joe Dublin, that money never showed up in Sureño. The town's merchants didn't benefit in any way from a mysterious increase in turnover, and you're not only an old man, you're a poor old man living on a spread falling down around his ears.'

Lloyd's smile was a thin split in dry paper. 'That doesn't make me poor. It simply means that for twenty years I've had no need to work for a living.'

'I wonder why that is. Somebody must have benefited from that train robbery. You've now as good as admitted it wasn't you, at least not directly, not in bundles of used banknotes—'

'Shut up.'

Jack's eyes widened with shock. The idea that the situation was under his control had been dealt a blow. Elgan Lloyd's frailty did not extend to his mind or his courage. He was facing a man with a six-gun, a man with reason to kill him, and was unfazed. It occurred to Jack that he might have walked into a trap. If not that, then certainly he had underestimated the opposition.

Through the cottonwood trees, he could see the steely shine of the river. The blood bay was there, grazing on the river's grassy banks, but the buckboard's driver had vanished from view – where was he? A hasty glance back along the trail added to Jack's worries. The dust thrown up by the buckboard's dash down the trail was settling slowly. The entrance to Tredegar was barely visible through it. Squint as he might into that hazed sunlight, Jack couldn't be sure if his eyes were playing tricks on him, or that the two riders had finished at the house and were about to follow the buckboard into town.

'You believe I'm in no position to give orders,' Lloyd said, watching him. 'What you fail to understand is that nobody cares what you believe. Of course I planned the robbery.'

'Why?'

Lloyd hesitated, licked dry lips, shook his head slowly from side to side.

'You were a reasonably successful man, Lloyd. I'd say you had a lot to lose. Yet you risked everything planning a robbery from which you got no immediate financial gain. That can lead to only one conclusion. Someone was holding a gun to your head, and I mean that figuratively. One possibility is a guilty secret. Your past had come up to haunt you; this feller was using it.'

'You can believe what you like,' Lloyd said, 'but it changes nothing. I planned the robbery, the men who stopped that train and used dynamite to blast their way into the armoured carriage all worked for me on the Tredegar ranch. And we got away with it, Garrison.'

'Good years can end. It's never too late for a reckoning.'

'Wrong. I'm telling you the truth now because you cannot touch us. Twenty years ago four men paid for that crime. The law, and the men running that railroad, were entirely satisfied. If you tried pointing the finger now at a nonagenarian and some grey-haired men with paunches, you'd be laughed out of town.' Lloyd chuckled throatily. 'Besides, if I can use a baseball term, you cannot even get to first base. Show your face, and you'll be arrested and sent back to prison.'

'That's if your men don't get to me first,' Garrison said. 'And if I can't touch you or them, why am I being hunted like a rabid dog?'

'At the risk of repeating myself, because you're an escaped prisoner.'

'There's more to it than that.' Garrison shook his head. 'I told you, someone's getting desperate. From what you've said it seems you got paid a pittance, spread over the years, and you accepted that because your hand was forced, you were blackmailed into committing a crime. Well, the man ruthless enough to do that is at it again. He got his money all right, but twenty years on from that robbery he's got so much to lose my escape's got him calling again on you and your—'

Garrison broke off.

The buckboard had rocked. In the same instant, he felt a sharp prick at the nape of his neck, the warm stickiness as the skin was broken and blood began to flow.

'Sending me walking without keeping your eye on me was a mistake, pal,' the buckboard's young driver said. 'Make a move now, and you'll be like a hog on a spit.'

'Just hold him like that,' Elgan Lloyd said, as he bent awkwardly and swept up the derringer. 'If you care to listen, Garrison, you'll hear me cocking this little pistol's hammer. You'll also hear the sound of horses. Your eyes did not deceive you: the two men I was talking to will be with us very shortly. From where I sit, I'd say you're looking at defeat from just about every imaginable direction.'

FOURTEEN

Jack Garrison knew he had to act, and act fast. To throw himself backwards away from the cocked pistol would see his head impaled on the driver's knife blade. Lloyd had an agile mind, but his body was a ruin. He was the weak link.

Garrison still had hold of his six-gun. He came off the seat in a lunge, his arm raised, and went for the old man. The flicker in Lloyd's eyes told him the old man had sent the signal to his finger to pull the derringer's trigger. His body let him down. The clawed right hand refused to cooperate; his reaction was that fraction too slow. Without hesitation, Garrison brought the six-gun down on the old man's head. The black felt of his hat helped to cushion the blow, but the light went out of the rheumy eyes and the jaw dropped open. He toppled backwards, went all the way out of the buckboard.

Before he had hit the ground Garrison had leaped over him and was sprinting for the woods. Old man Lloyd was out of it, possibly dead. The driver had been holding a knife. His gunbelt was on the floor. He would go for that, or the inevitable shotgun – but both moves took time. As for the riders down the trail, they were entering the cloud of settling dust and would find visibility hampered. From afar they would have seen the buckboard pulled in under the trees, but the shadows cast by the high sun would add to their difficulties. They'd see movement, squint into the light and shade, belatedly catch rapid movement and the glint of flashing gunmetal, and put spurs to their horses.

But Jack Garrison was getting away.

The blood bay had not strayed far. It was still grazing, moving slowly along the river-bank. Garrison took the direct route through the trees, ripping aside snagging undergrowth that clawed at his knees, ducking beneath the sharp white of stubs of broken branches, using arms and elbows to brush aside springy, whipping saplings. His eyes were on the way ahead; his ears were listening for the roar of a shotgun, the snick of lead shot tearing through leaves. But he had the advantage. The stand of trees was at once an obstacle and a shield, slowing him down when he craved speed, but making the chance of buckshot or bullets hitting him highly unlikely.

He reached the other side of the cottonwood gasping for breath, sprang out into bright sunlight and whistled shrilly for the bay. It cocked its ears, saw him, and came trotting along the bank with stirrups flapping, reins trailing. Garrison ran to meet it.

He almost got there. Then a horse came galloping around the edge of the woods in a hard, tight turn. The rider had a six-gun in his hand. He was leaning out of the saddle, into the curve, using his weight to balance the horse. Even so, its hoofs slipped from under it as they went from the firmness of hard-packed earth to treacherous moist grass. The horse slithered and went down hard on its side, sliding, snorting, eyes wild as its hoofs flailed in the air. The rider tried to kick his feet free of the stirrups but the one underneath the horse had got tangled; his leg was pinned by the horse's weight. As the horse kicked, thrashed, the rider cast a wild look in Garrison's direction. He'd lost his pistol in the fall. It lay yards away in the grass. He flung out an arm but his hand slapped earth far short of the weapon. Desperately, he rammed his free foot against the saddle and thrust hard with his leg muscles. His trapped leg began to slide free.

Then a second horse came around the trees. It saw the downed horse at the last moment, cut sharply away and almost came a cropper. As the rider struggled to stay in the saddle the horse reared, took the bit between its teeth and the easy way out: it galloped down the slope towards the river.

At the same time, the buckboard's driver, following fast on Garrison's heels, came crashing out of the undergrowth. He was holding a shotgun, waist high. His eyes fastened on Garrison. He brought the gun up, began to swing it into the aim.

The circus had come to town, and all its crazy action had taken place in the merest blink of an eye. Garrison had not yet slowed his run, nor did he now. He was acutely aware of the kid with the scattergun and of the trapped man freeing himself and flapping at his fallen six-gun as he rolled clear of the horse. Expecting at any moment to be blasted to bloody shreds, he reached the bay, grabbed the horn and swung himself into the saddle.

His intention had been to race back down the river towards Sureño, but the noise of the turmoil had startled the big horse and it had turned. Facing the wrong way for a fast getaway, it was trembling with fright. Or maybe, Garrison thought, the way it's facing is the right way to go. Pile chaos on chaos. Confuse by doing the unexpected. So thinking, he kicked the horse from standstill to a bounding run and drove it hard for the end of the trees.

The riderless horse was back on its feet. Unsteady, looking around wildly, it broke into an aimless trot. The unseated rider grabbed for the trailing reins, missed, and the horse cut across in front of the racing bay. Before Garrison could react the big horse veered sharply away from the riderless horse. The new line took it perilously close to the trees. Thick overhanging branches threatened to unseat Garrison.

Then, as he flattened himself along the bay's neck to avoid being decapitated, from behind him there came a thunderous roar. The kid had got the shotgun lined up. Lead pellets hissed, but well above Garrison's exposed back. His instinctive reaction to the overhanging branches had saved his life. There was a second blast as the kid fired the other barrel, then a series of lighter cracks as the man who'd been unhorsed opened fire with his six-gun.

The horse that had bolted towards the river had been brought under control. With angry curses and tight reins the rider had managed to turn it and kick it into a run. He was riding hard back up the slope, threatening to cut off Garrison's escape.

It was Geraint Lloyd. He grinned savagely, spurred the horse to greater speed. Garrison had thirty yards to go before he could swing around the end of the stand of cottonwoods. Knowing he had no chance of making it, he took the only course open to him. Swinging the big blood bay in a tight turn to the left, he took it crashing into the trees.

Behind him, Geraint Lloyd yelled his fury. Bullets whistled over Garrison's head as Lloyd began snapping wild shots. But at that point the woods had thinned, and there was little undergrowth. The bay's raking strides took it through swiftly, and it burst into the open in dazzling sunlight.

They were some yards behind the buckboard. Elgan Lloyd was up on his feet but leaning against the wagon like a man the worse for drink. His thin face was like a death mask, his eyes like the marks of fingers poked in snow. One hand was gripping the buckboard's side rail. From the other the tiny derringer pistol dangled.

Knowing he was clear now, and running free, Garrison avoided him. He swept the bay wide around the wagon's tail gate, heard two sharp snaps as the game old man emptied the derringer in his direction. Then he was off the grass and heading at speed down the trail towards town.

106

He fully expected a hot pursuit. But a hasty glance over his shoulder showed Geraint Lloyd pulling his horse alongside his father and swinging out of the saddle. Of the other rider, and the wagon's young driver, there was no sign.

Pulling the bay back to an easy canter, Garrison relaxed in the saddle, took a moment to wipe the sweat from his brow, waited for his breathing to settle. He was riding in the general direction of Sureño, but for him the town was out of bounds. Once again he was going to have to turn south towards the Mohawk foothills, before again swinging east.

The sun was almost overhead. It was, he estimated, close to midday. He and Rick going their separate ways had seemed like a good idea, but together they might have turned the situation at the river to their advantage – though it was difficult to see how. What he had heard from Elgan Lloyd had convinced him that it was useless hounding the old man, but had told him nothing about the man behind him; the man who, twenty years ago, had been desperate for money.

The one crumb of comfort was that in the darkness of night he and Rick would come together again at Poco a Poco Creek. In the meantime, all Jack could do was lie low.

FIFTEEN

That night, the moon was veiled by thin, high cloud, creating an eerie landscape through which Jack Garrison rode like a phantom horseman. The banjo was again across his back, the animal skin head a grey disk that appeared to cling to him like the ghost of the absent moon. Well clear of town, Jack rode down from the foothills where he had spent half the day and a part of the evening and cut across the trail towards Poco a Poco Creek.

He held his rifle across his thighs. The morning's action had looked like a circus act put on by clowns, but he was not deceived. The truth was that all the chaos had been caused by one horse losing its footing, and even then he had been lucky to get away. Elgan Lloyd's men were not fools. Without doubt, a determined pursuit would have caught Jack. Instead, Lloyd had held his men back. There had to be a reason.

One possibility was that he had decided Rick Garrison was an easier target. Younger than Jack, not tormented by memories of twenty years in a penitentiary, vulnerable because as a clean-living ex-town marshal he had more to lose. So as he came up off the trail onto the small flat plateau bisected by the dry creek bed, Jack was prepared for the possibility that Rick could have been followed.

Prepared, but not unduly worried.

Although a rifleman had opened up when Garrison was at the creek with Joe Dublin, he had been forced to plug away from a distance because the area around Poco a Poco was too flat and barren to make an ambush feasible. The only cover available in the immediate vicinity was provided by the cottonwoods down by the Gila River where, what seemed like years ago, Garrison had tethered the blood bay. On the plateau even a lone bushwhacker would have had difficulty finding concealment, and the truth of that was borne out when Jack caught sight of the horse. It was at the back of the flat ground – again a familiar spot, for Jack had sat there smoking a cigarette while awaiting the arrival of Joe Dublin.

But even as he relaxed and bent to slip the rifle into the boot under his left thigh, he realized something was wrong. All the time they had been together Rick had been riding a sorrel. The horse waiting patiently, ground-tethered, was a dun gelding powerful enough to pull a plough.

Instead of pouching the rifle, Jack brought it back up, fast. As he did so he slid out of the saddle – a lizard, there, then gone. He kept the blood bay between him and the big dun. Using the horse's body as a living shield, he relaxed his knees so that only his hat and eyes were exposed above the saddle. Heart thumping, he let his eyes range, probing the shadows.

Nothing. Was the rider there? Or had he left the horse and walked away. Was he even now down in the cover of the cottonwoods, taking his time lining up his rifle, rejoicing in the fact that the banjo across Jack's back gave him a target impossible to miss.

The big dun whickered softly. The blood bay stirred restlessly.

Out in the open, his mouth dry, Jack Garrison waited for the bullet that would put a violent end to his search for justice.

SIXTEEN

Around noon on that same day, at about the time Jack Garrison was racing away from the Lloyd buckboard, Rick Garrison was also settling down to a meal in Sureño's only café. Most of that morning had been spent a mile or three to the south of the town, lazing in the shade of a stand of trees, smoking one cigarette after another. But he was not a man accustomed to inactivity, and growing hunger pains made him decide to brazen it out and ride boldly into town. Officially he was still the town's marshal, and that thought brought a grin to his face as he flicked away his cigarette, swung a leg over his buckskin, and set off down the hill.

Nothing had happened, he reasoned, that could not be explained. And why, after all, should a town marshal be obliged to explain his actions? He set his mind to work on that premise as he rode towards Sureño.

In the middle of the night, one man had seen him walk out of the jail with the prisoner, Jack Garrison. They had been conversing, unhurried, going nowhere in haste. Rick's comments to the man who had spotted them had been jocular, but firm; he was the familiar town marshal, telling a falling-down drunk to go home to bed.

The next day, Jack Garrison had still been with him; the town marshal still had his prisoner. Then, on the slopes of the foothills, the two of them had fought off men intent on murder and escaped with their lives. Those men and their actions, Rick could stress, confirmed his justification in taking Jack Garrison from jail: he had heard rumours, and been concerned for the prisoner's safety.

The fact that the prisoner was no longer with him was, well, unfortunate, difficult to explain, but that too could be worked on.

His thinking, it seemed, had been inspired. Town was bustling. When Rick rode in he had made damn sure that his badge was on his vest, shining in the sunlight. He waved and smiled at acquaintances, rode as close as he could to the jail. Raker's horse was at the hitch rail. The deputy himself was in the doorway. He nearly fell over when he saw Rick.

'Going for a bite to eat,' Rick called, and he waved in the direction of the café. 'You OK to hold the fort?'

All Raker could do was nod numbly. Rick hadn't looked back but, nearing the end of his meal, he was still wondering how long the deputy had stood there, struck dumb.

The answer to that came in such an unexpected way that it was his turn temporarily to lose the power of speech.

He had pushed his plate away and was settling back to enjoy a cigarette with his second cup of coffee when the cow bell over the door clanked. Two men came in. Both were tall, lean, with restless eyes and right hands that brushed the butts of identical six-guns. Their well-cut black, broad-cloth suits were trail dusty.

There were three men at tables in the café. The newcomers gave them the briefest of glances, then took one look at Rick and headed his way. Raker had recovered composure fast, Rick thought bitterly, had told them where to find him and given them a description. What he didn't know was who these men were. Then, as they reached his table, split up, and placed themselves either side of him, he saw what he'd missed.

Pinned to their vests were United States Federal Marshal shields.

And all at once it became clear that by using a stick to stir up a small southern town, he and Jack had lit a fire under the tail of a sleeping tiger in the state's capitol.

One of the marshals spoke. For all the emotion in his voice he might have been addressing a fly he's just squashed.

'Rick Garrison?'

Like Raker before him, Rick could only nod numbly.

'We'd like you to come with us, Garrison. Voluntarily would save face, but it's up to you.'

They followed him across the street to the jail, letting him walk ahead without restraint because, as Rick knew full well, they were confident in their ability to kill him stone dead if he made a break. He could feel their cold eyes on his back, see in his mind's eye their hands poised over the worn butts of their six-guns.

He'd set his mind to working on how to handle the unexpected when he walked out of the café. It didn't take him long. He'd come down from the hills confident in the authority of his office. Nothing had happened since then to make him change course.

So, ignoring the two marshals, he ran boldly up the steps and into the jail office. Raker was sprawled in the swivel chair behind the desk.

'Out,' Rick said, hooking a thumb.

The response was a sneer.

Rick took two swift strides, grabbed the deputy by the throat and threw him bodily to the floor. Raker rolled, swore a filthy oath, and went for his gun. Rick let him pull it, then kicked it out of his hand. He grabbed the man's shirt collar, dragged him kicking away from the desk. When he dropped into the vacant swivel chair, his breathing was normal.

'As of now,' he said, 'you're out of a job, Raker. Drop your badge on the desk on your way out. If you can't walk, crawl.'

Under the amused gaze of the marshals, Raker climbed to his feet. His face was purple. He looked for his gun, saw where it had clattered against the wall, mouthed another curse and went for it.

'Leave it where it is. Go sit down.'

The marshal giving the order walked easily to the wall by the window, leaned against it with legs crossed, lit a cigarette. He watched dispassionately as Raker glowered, hesitated, then with reluctance dropped into a chair where he sat smouldering with anger. The marshal's colleague found another chair, swivelled it, and sat astride with his arms folded on the back.

'My name's Rome,' he said to Rick. 'The feller looking deceptively relaxed by the window's Miller, and you'll understand I'm being polite here; the names don't mean a damn. All you need to know is the badge I'm wearing makes me God. All you need to do is tell me where we can find your brother. That way, instead of facing a full life sentence in Yuma you can be looking at an easy ten years.'

Raker's chuckle was venomous. 'You can be sure his brother's told him that in Yuma there's no such thing as easy time.'

'I won't be doing *any* time,' Rick said. 'As town marshal I'm responsible for my prisoner. His life was in danger.'

'You act righteous, but last night you opened the cell door,' Rome said, 'and walked an escaped convict out of your jail.'

'I've just told you why. Even a convicted man has rights, can expect protection. This morning, up on the mountain, men working for Elgan Lloyd tried to kill us. That made moving my prisoner from jail the right decision.'

'So where is he now?'

'Telling you would be telling him.' Rick jerked his head at Raker, who was watching from the other side of the office. 'Telling him would be like telling Lloyd.'

'Lloyd? Who the hell is this Lloyd?'

'For Christ's sake—'

'I'd say you don't know where your brother is. I'd say you let him go. That was a *wrong* decision.'

'A jail's not the only place a man can be held under lock and key for his own good,' Rick said. 'And here's a thought you can chew on: if that badge makes you God, why do you need me to tell you where he is?'

The marshal called Miller stirred, wandered away from

the window and over to the gun rack. Absently, he ran a finger down a shiny rifle barrel. 'It's time you stopped playing games,' he said, his back to Rick. 'If you've got him safe somewhere, take us to him now. Do that, and maybe we'll forget all about last night; you go back to being marshal in a lazy southern town.'

'I'm not a fool,' Rick said. 'I know there's much more to this than a prisoner on the run from Yuma.'

Rome cocked an eyebrow. 'More?'

'This is about a train robbery, an innocent man being framed. You can't let either one of us stay free, because the cork's been pulled, the genie's out of the bottle. Elgan Lloyd and his ageing train robbers have had it too easy for too long. Somewhere out there is the big man behind the whole damn shebang. Lloyd's keeping that big man's name under his hat. Christ only knows who he is, but Jack's got him rattled. Your presence here makes it clear he called for official help. The fact that he could do that tells me he's got considerable influence in high places.'

Rome stood up, spun the chair out of his way. Miller stopped admiring the rack of rifles and turned to face the room. His eyes locked with Rome's. Rome grimaced, spread his hands, frowned at Rick.

'There's that name Lloyd again,' he said. 'And what's all that nonsense about a big man?' He looked at Raker as if for enlightenment, and shook his head. 'You've got me baffled, Garrison. We're here because a convict serving life for robbery and the killing of three train guards walked out of the state penitentiary and is running rings around the local law.'

116

'So you two are from Yuma?'

Again the marshals exchanged glances.

'No, we're from Phoenix,' Miller said. 'This has nothing to do with anyone called Lloyd, it was the prison warden asked for help.'

Rick shook his head. 'Now I *know* you're lying. The warden would send his own armed men from Yuma, not call for two fancy Dans from the state capitol.'

'You know nothing—'

'Another thing,' Rick cut in. 'The name Rome rings a bell. I've heard it, but damned if I can remember where.'

There was a silence in the room. Suddenly Rome was staring hard at Rick. Then Miller let go an explosive, exasperated breath.

'We're getting nowhere,' he said to Rome. 'He's not going to give up his brother.'

'What do you suggest?'

'I'll leave that to you. Whatever you think is for the best.'

'Then we let him go.'

Again looks were exchanged. Rome smiled. Miller nodded, looked at Rick.

'You heard him. I can understand your loyalty to your brother, but it's finished you as a lawman. Throw your badge down, and walk out of here now before Rome changes his mind.'

'I'll walk out, but I keep my badge.'

Miller shrugged. Waited.

Rick swung the swivel chair and came out of it in a rush. When he walked around the desk and strode towards the door, Raker had straightened in his chair. His dark eyes looked at Rome, at Rick Garrison's retreating back, and his face was split by a cruel grin. A crime he'd thought dead and buried had been resurrected by Jack Garrison and was threatening to drag him and others involved down into deep mire. A man who saw everything in life as pure black and white, Raker knew the only solution to their problem was to get rid of the Garrison brothers.

Rick was a pace or two from the open air when Marshal Rome casually drew his six-gun from leather and shot him in the back of the head. Rick dropped like a stone, dead before he hit the dirt floor.

The gunshot's reverberations were like the sound of distant thunder. When they faded to nothing, the silence was the silence of the grave.

'Did you see that?' Rome said.

'The man went for his gun,' Raker said. 'He was making a break for it, resisting arrest.'

Rome grinned at him. 'Congratulations, feller. You just got yourself promoted marshal of Sureño.'

Raker's face was grim. His eyes on Rick Garrison's body, on the thin trickle of blood under the dead man's head, he said, 'I didn't like the man, know damn well he had to go, but I worked with him all my life—'

'Not true.' Rome was shaking his head. 'You worked with him during the time he was in office here. If you play your cards right, you're going to live to be as old as Elgan Lloyd.'

'I thought you didn't know Lloyd?'

'Thinking's not your job.'

Rome threw a glance at the dead man lying in the sunlight flooding in through the open door, a harder glare at the horrified men and women in the street who hurried away when they met his cold gaze.

He turned away, looked at Miller and said thoughtfully, 'Lloyd and his crew are wilting like corn in a drought. Jack Garrison's the exact opposite and that makes him dangerous.'

'More so now,' Raker said, 'with his kid brother lying dead on the ground.'

'But both those problems need settling,' Rome said. 'The way I see it, Rick Garrison can still be useful.'

'A dead body, in the right place, can put the fear of God in a man,' Miller said, cottoning on fast.

'Needs a little hard work in the dead of night,' Rome said. He grinned at Raker. 'You up for it?'

'I don't understand.'

'Just say yes. It'll be your salvation. There's a minor war being fought, and that feller lying there is going to make parties on both sides take a long hard look at their future prospects.'

SEVENTEEN

In the shadows beyond the patient dun gelding, a cigarette end glowed. A second later it spun away through the air, a firefly followed by a shower of lesser lights. When the man who'd flicked away the cigarette stood up, the reason for the powerful horse became clear. Jack Garrison felt his shoulders creak as tension leaked away. So strong was the sense of relief that he threw back his head and laughed out loud.

'I was expecting my brother,' he said, 'but you'll do for now.'

'Forget for now, it could be much longer than that.'

It was Ed Corcoran, the burly blacksmith. Emerging from the shadows, he patted his horse and waved a vague hand towards Sureño. 'Last I saw of Rick he was being marched across the street from the café by a couple of tough-looking characters with a lot of swagger. Woman in the café said she'd been listening. Her impression was they were lawmen from Phoenix.'

'Why Phoenix?'

'These are big boys, a big step up from any two-bit law we've got in Sureño. One glance'll tell you they're lawmen at the top of a very tall tree, used to wearing smart suits, looking down their noses at lesser folk. Way I see it, if you were still town marshal, you'd be one of the small fry. Someone's sent them in, Garrison, and it's you they're after. Maybe old Elgan Lloyd figured he was getting nowhere and appealed for help. What's more likely is the big man pulling strings lost patience.'

'What the hell do you know about a big man?'

'There's nobody in Sureño could have planned that train robbery—'

'You've lost me, Corcoran.'

'Nobody,' Corcoran went on, 'you could hurt bad, so there has to be another reason for all the ruckus.'

Jack nodded slowly. He'd kept the bay between him and Corcoran, leaning on the saddle as he talked. Now he came around the horse. Lost in thought, he rolled a cigarette, lit it, tossed the makings to the blacksmith.

'Assuming you know what you're talking about,' he said at last, 'I'd say this big man who's pulling strings got complacent. The years rolled by. He figured he was clear, home and dry. Then one night a man came over a prison wall, opened a can of worms, and now he's desperate.'

'But why should that be?' Corcoran asked. A match flared as he lit his cigarette. 'Hell, everyone in Sureño knows what you're looking for, and up to now what have you got? You've been runnin' around like a chicken who lost his head twenty years ago, and you're not even close to an answer.'

121

'Closer now,' Jack said. 'Panic can lead to desperate measures. By sending in the marshals our friend in high places has turned over a hole card, revealed too much.'

'And maybe issued a stark warning, Garrison.'

'Warnings are wasted on a man with nothing to lose.'

'If he's got family, the poorest man alive has got something to lose,' Corcoran said, and he squinted at Jack through the cigarette smoke, let the thought hang in the still night air, gathering meaning and menace.

'You mean Rick?' Jack said. 'He won't give anything away to those marshals, that's for sure. And from riding with him – even though it's been for little more than half a day – I know he can look after himself.'

'The law's too big to fight, Jack. Got long arms, and government backing.'

'And I'll deal with that,' Jack said as he flicked away his half-finished cigarette. 'But first we come to you, Corcoran. I saw you in your workshop, next thing is you're in the saloon dealing Joe Dublin a knockout blow. Why?'

'Because he was dangerous as a wounded cougar, and I need you.'

'What use could I be to you, a stranger?'

'You were never a stranger. I had you pegged from the start. You'd come to me asking questions about a *friend* name of Rick Garrison, but you were looking at me with his eyes. I'd lived twenty years without hope, and damned if Jack Garrison, one of the four train robbers, didn't walk bold as brass into my forge.'

'If you believe that—'

'I don't, though others will. But listen to me. Three of

the robbers, they were hanged – right?'

'That's a rumour got lost in time.'

'The only rumour was in the men's identity. No train robbers were hanged. I knew a guard in Yuma, because I was a regular visitor. He told me how three men were taken from the penitentiary to those aspen woods, hanged there, and a suitable story cooked up.' Corcoran paused. 'Two were convicted murderers,' he went on, 'so in that sense they were no loss.'

'I can see where this is going,' Jack said. 'If you were a regular visitor at the Yuma pen...?'

'You've got it. The third man hanged was my father,' Corcoran said. 'He was caught red-handed branding stolen cattle—'

'Hell fire, I remember the name now. He was one of the men with Geraint Lloyd.'

'Right. It was you arrested the bunch of them. My pa was older, so they figured he was the leader and he drew more time than young Lloyd. He was about due for release, but on that day they badly needed a third man to hang.'

'Jesus Christ,' Jack said softly. 'And all this … this cold-blooded murder done in the name of justice goes back to a train robbery, and the man who ordered it carried out.'

'We both of us waited twenty years,' Corcoran said. 'Much of what we're saying is still down to guesswork. But it's educated guesswork leading, in my opinion, to the only possible answer. If I have my way, and there is a big man out there who caused all that pain and suffering, we'll get to him and he'll spend the rest of his life in prison.' His grin was savage. 'And it would be even more fitting if they took him to Yuma in chains and locked him up in my pa's old cell.'

EIGHTEEN

For Jack Garrison, the news of his brother's arrest by lawmen from Phoenix dealt a serious blow to his immediate plans – such as they were. The involvement of marshals from the state capitol might suggest he had the man behind the train robbery gnawing his fingernails with worry, but it changed his priorities. He could go no further in his hunt for the big man until Rick was free. As he couldn't show his face in Sureño without getting arrested, or shot down as a dangerous escaped convict, achieving that seemed like an impossible task.

Drinking copious quantities of strong coffee brewed in a blackened pot over a smokeless fire, he and Ed Corcoran talked half the night away. A lot was nostalgic reminiscing, even though they were of different ages and with different backgrounds. Some was talk of that long ago train robbery, and speculation on who had benefited. Most was thrashing away at the problem of Rick's arrest. The action they eventually settled on was obvious, even if only a partial solution. They would ride into town. Jack would stay hidden. Under some as yet undecided pretext, Ed Corcoran would wander across and poke his nose into the jail.

When the first thin slivers of dawn were still a vague promise below the eastern horizon, they stowed the cups and other paraphernalia in saddle-bags and set off for Sureño. The horses had been asleep on their feet, and so were sluggish for the first couple of miles, then wide awake and eager to run with their hoofs kicking up dust and breath flaring white in the cool morning air.

The town was a sprawl of dark buildings, poking roofs and false fronts through the low hanging river mist. The oil lamps hanging over the main street's plank walks glowed dimly, casting weak light no further than the walls of the buildings, the uprights and brush roofs of the *ramadas*.

'Make your way along the river, come up the alley opposite the jail,' Corcoran said as they rode in. 'Wait there. I'll check on those Phoenix boys. Not yet dawn, I reckon they'll still have their heads down somewhere, but we'll see. If they're there in the jail they won't bother me, a simple blacksmith with his brains in his hands. If they're not....'

Jack nodded agreement. He'd used that same littered alleyway when heading off to talk to Elgan Lloyd. He rode briskly away from Corcoran, the cold of the Gila's waters a chill on his right side. When, after a half mile or so, he brought the big blood bay up from the river and between the buildings, Corcoran was across the street and entering the jail.

Deep in shadow, Jack stuck a cigarette in his mouth, scraped a match and cupped his hands around the flame. He sat easy in the saddle, smoking, gazing across at the jail's open door, at two shapes moving in the ill-lit room.

Then Corcoran's bulky figure was in the doorway, waving him across.

Jack flicked away the unfinished cigarette. He rode fast across the street, swung down from the saddle and leaped up onto the plank walk without tethering his horse. Movement in the jail's office told him the second shape he'd seen was Raker. The blacksmith was still in the doorway, now backing out of Jack's way. But as he did so, grim-faced, he pointed to a section of the dirt floor close to the door.

The stain was a dark reddish-brown. Dried blood. But not long dry. Without asking, Jack knew the blood was his brother's. Rick was dead.

Feeling a numbness creep over him, he shook his head. He stepped into the room, avoiding the stain. Corcoran's big hand closed on his arm, steadying him before Jack realized he had swayed like a sapling in the breeze.

He looked at Raker. Sureño's new marshal was standing by the desk. The badge on his vest had belonged to Rick Garrison. Once, long ago, to Jack. Raker's stance was awkward, the look on his face uneasiness verging on the downright scared.

'What happened?'

Raker grimaced, licked his lips. 'Rick was questioned, they let him walk, then shot him down in cold blood. Back of the head. One shot. The man was called Rome.

127

Resisting arrest was the excuse, but that was a pure lie.'

'When?'

Raker spread his hands. 'Yesterday afternoon, some time.'

'You were here?'

'Sitting right there.' Raker pointed to a chair.

'And where are they now?'

'Christ knows. They stepped over his body. Rome tripped, laughed at himself, then gave the … gave the body a kick. They walked out of here. Said nothing then, because they'd said it all between shooting and leaving.'

He grimaced, hesitating. To Jack it seemed that Raker was bracing himself to deliver bad news. But what could be worse than the cold-blooded killing of a good man?

'Said what? And what happened to Rick? There's nothing left here but some of his blood, so where is he? The undertaker come for him?'

Raker swallowed. He shook his head, no.

'Then where?'

Still Raker stood as if struck dumb.

'Come on, man,' Corcoran snarled.

'I dragged Rick inside, out of the sun. Shut the door. Kept him out back in the cool of the cells for the rest of the day. That was what they told me to do. Rome had plans, a big idea. Said he and his pal would come back after dark. Told me what we'd do with him, with Rick. Said it was heavy work, would need the three of us.'

'Jesus Christ,' Jack said softly, wonderingly, his mind reeling at undreamed of horrors.

'I've had a bellyful,' Raker said, suddenly decisive,

128

gaining in confidence.

Or was that an act? Jack wondered. Had Raker been performing for their benefit from the moment they walked in the door? Was he pulling their strings, even now following instructions given by the lawmen from Phoenix?

Watching him, Raker pushed away from the desk.

'You'd best come with me.'

The dawn was yellow.

At certain times of the Arizona year there would be an excess of dust in the atmosphere. Mostly it was after a storm. Sometimes it just happened. It was one of those days. The sun came up behind a haze that touched the horizon in all directions, a filter that made a mockery of daylight and deprived men of shadows. Grass, whether lush or parched, lost its colour. The Gila River flowed in a sulphurous stream, so quiet that it was as if the strange overcast deadened sound.

Rick Garrison's body was hanging from the heavy timber crossbeam marking the entrance to Tredegar, the spread owned by Elgan Lloyd. He was suspended head down, by a rope tied around his ankles. His arms dangled, fingertips almost touching the dust of the trail. The breeze that had sprung up and begun dissipating the mist and the haze was moving the body gently from side to side, a grotesque pendulum.

Jack Garrison muttered something unintelligible, leaped down from the blood roan and reached up to hold still his brother's body. Corcoran stayed in the saddle. He rode close, took out a knife and stood in the stirrups. When the rope was cut, Jack wrapped his arms around the body and held it, eased it down it until he could take the weight and laid his brother on the hard ground.

It was only then, when Corcoran was out of the saddle and he and Jack stood, white of face, over the dead man, that they realized their every movement had been watched.

It was the first time Jack had seen old man Lloyd on horseback.

He was dressed as he had been when accosted by Jack in the buckboard, but now he was a diminutive, bent figure astride an aging chestnut thoroughbred. In the intense glare as the rising sun banished the last of the strange mist, his face was a white mask through which black eyes glistened like shards of wet coal. He was alone. As still as a life-sized statue that might have been carved from a block of mahogany to mark the entrance to Tredegar.

'I heard something,' he said, his voice a dry rasp. 'Horses. Men talking. I don't sleep too well.'

'Damn right you don't,' Jack Garrison said. 'It would surprise me if you've had one good night's sleep in twenty years.'

'From my room I can see all of this.' He waved a hand vaguely, at the trail, at the uprights, and at the massive crossbeam from which Rick Garrison had been suspended. 'I have field glasses, from the war years. I saw everything.'

'The everything you saw no longer matters. You know what I need from you. Tell me the name of the man who's been paying you for twenty years.'

'If I did that,' Lloyd said, 'those payments would end.'

'Rest assured, Lloyd, they're going to end, and very soon. The men who killed my brother are US marshals from Phoenix. Whoever sent them made a big mistake. Before that I was in the dark. Now I'm seeing some light—'

'Jack!'

Corcoran's voice was sharp, urgent. Jack spun, took in the situation at a glance. They had forgotten Raker. While Jack had been talking to Lloyd the Sureño lawman had ridden back across the trail. Now, hearing Corcoran's warning shout, he used spurs to send his horse bounding through the coarse grass of the verge and into the safety of the trees.

As if that was a signal previously arranged, two rifles opened up from the stands of trees further up the trail towards Yuma.

Jack was saved by the nearest timber upright.

The first bullets sent sharp splinters flying, whirring away into the hot air like hornets in a hurry.

He had walked forward to face up to Lloyd. That had put the upright between him and the unseen gunmen. Now, pressing up close with his back hard against the wood, he flashed a hand to his holster and drew his six-gun. Waited for a lull in the shooting, a chance to return fire. Which he knew full well would be a waste of time

131

and bullets. The range was too great for him to hit any target smaller than a barn door.

But the gunmen were ignoring Corcoran, concentrating on Jack, the man causing all the trouble. And, given that breathing space, the big blacksmith took full advantage. He was still close to his horse. As the first bullets began flying he ducked down and slid his rifle out of the saddle-boot. He was just in time, but too late to make a grab for Jack's '73 Winchester. Spooked, his sorrel and Jack's roan fled, ears back, tails hoisted like flags of distress. Jack heard the blacksmith curse softly as he made a lunge across the yards of open ground and got his body behind the other massive upright. He dropped to one knee, brought the rifle up, risked a quick look up the trail.

As he did so, bullets began to hiss in from the other direction. Raker had joined the fray. Suddenly they were caught in a vicious crossfire. Avoiding Raker's bullets would give the other gunmen clear targets. And, Jack Garrison thought grimly, now was surely the time for old man Lloyd to pull his rifle from its worn saddle-boot. One bullet would end all Jack's hopes, leave Elgan Lloyd comfortable for what was left of his life.

A time that proved to be measurable in seconds.

Perhaps the old man sensed he was looking death in the face. He had backed up his horse as the bullets began to fly. One swift glance from Jack told him that Lloyd was preparing, with difficulty, to turn and get the hell out of there. He was still working his horse when the firing stopped. Abruptly. There was an eerie silence in which all that could be heard was a high ringing in the ears.

Then, from up the trail, a cry rang out.

'Give it up, Garrison. Throw down your gun and walk out onto the trail with your hands up. A prison cell for life is better than death.'

'Identify yourself.'

'Rome, Phoenix marshal.'

'You're a disgrace, Rome. A killer, not a respectable upholder of the law. My educated guess is you and your partner have run out of rifle shells. You're too damn cowardly to risk facing me and Corcoran with six-guns, so you're looking for the easy option.'

There was a harsh laugh. Then a single shot rang out. Without a sound, old man Lloyd tumbled from the saddle. There was a crack of old, brittle bones breaking as he hit the hard ground. He lay without moving.

'There's my answer,' Rome called. 'I'm waiting for yours.'

Jack flicked a glance at Corcoran. The big blacksmith grimaced.

'They aim to bury anything to do with that old train robbery. Lloyd planned it. Raker was one of those did the deed. He's taking their side, but doesn't realize he's likely to end up like your brother and the old man.'

'And us, if we don't act fast.'

'That won't happen. I'll give covering fire, keep their heads down. See if you can run along that fence, get close enough to make hitting something with your six-gun more than a stroke of luck.'

'And all this in a hurry, before Geraint Lloyd comes

down from the house.'

'If he does, those Phoenix boys'll make damn sure he's the next train robber to bite the dust.'

The fence stretched along the trail from the big upright, a line of rotting posts, rusting wire. Figuring the posts provided better cover than none at all, Jack stepped inside the Tredegar property. Then, bracing himself, he nodded to Corcoran.

The blacksmith worked the rifle's lever like a man born with a gun in his big hands. Shells slammed into the breech. The bullets flew fast and furious, the fusillade of hot lead clipping through the trees sheltering the lawmen some way up the trail. Garrison set off at a crouching run. He heard one of the marshals yell, either in anger or pain. No shots came his way. His hope was that Corcoran was keeping their heads so low they were blind to his progress and eating grass. He made thirty yards, fifty. Then Corcoran stopped to reload. Across the trail, one of the marshals risked standing up. He had taken his hat off. Dark of hair, he shot a swift glance towards the ranch entrance. Saw Corcoran bent over his rifle, the fresh shells glinting.

He raised his rifle.

Garrison had moved fast. He was level with their position. Panting, he stepped up to the fence. He fired two fast shots before the lawman could work the trigger. The crack of shots on his flank alerted the marshal to the danger. But it was too late. He half turned towards Garrison. Then his eyes widened, rolled. One of Jack's bullets had gone in under his raised arm and punctured his heart. Already he was going down. The rifle fell from his hands. There was a crackle of undergrowth. A sudden stillness.

Then Corcoran opened up again. But he'd been watching Garrison. Figuring Jack was in control, he turned and directed his fire at Raker. Watching, Jack knew his aim had been deadly, that the marshal was down. Corcoran was up on his feet, running without too much haste across the trail to the Sureño lawman's position.

Then, across from Jack Garrison, the second Phoenix marshal stepped out onto the trail. He tossed his rifle aside, grinned at Garrison, and went for his six-gun. He was tall, lean, and fast. But so was Garrison. He was working the trigger before the marshal's rifle had hit the ground. Yet even that was not fast enough. As he drew his gun the tall marshal was jinking to one side. Jack's first shot went wide; his second was closer but the target had again shifted.

Jack's third pull on the trigger brought nothing but a metallic click.

His six-gun was empty.

A quick, risky glance to his left told him that, fifty yards away, Corcoran was heading into the trees after Raker. No help from that direction. And the tall marshal was coming at Jack across the trail, a slow walk because now there was no rush, no danger. The grin was still in place, broader if anything as he anticipated shooting down an unarmed man, swatting away the second of the Garrison brothers like he would an annoying fly.

Jack flung the empty six-gun at his head.

His mind anticipating the cold-blooded killing to come, this time the marshal was too slow. The six-gun hit him in the face. The metal was heavy, with sharp edges. He stumbled backwards, blood streaming from his nose. Jack grabbed the rusty wire and threw himself over the fence. He was on the marshal before the thrown six-gun hit the ground. He hit him twice, a crunching blow to the damaged face, a second that sank into the lean midriff.

They were mighty punches, delivered with all the weight of his shoulders. But the tall, wiry marshal was strong, a fighter, a barroom brawler. His head rocked to the first punch. The second caused him to fold in the middle. But he absorbed the ferocious onslaught. His brain was working on a response. His hand holding the six-gun's butt had dropped as pain knifed through his face and brought tears to his eyes. Now it came up in a looping swing. The gun hit Jack a cruel blow above his ear but the brim of his Stetson cushioned it. Conscious but dazed, he was knocked off his feet.

He went down hard. The strength had leaked from his muscles. He shook his head, through unfocused eyes saw the grin had been wiped from the marshal's bloody face. The lazy anticipation was gone. Now the naked hatred in the man's eyes told of the urge to kill. He dragged a forearm across his face, cleared away the blood that was forcing him to breathe open-mouthed. Again he lifted the six-gun. His thumb cocked the hammer. The muzzle swung to point at Jack—

A rifle cracked.

The bullet hit the marshal in the shoulder.

His eyes registered shock. He sank to his knees, moaned, steadied himself with his pistol hand on the ground. Gritting his teeth, Jack gathered what strength he could and swung a wild kick. His boot took the marshal under the chin. The lawman's hat fell off, his head snapped back. He fell on his side, seemed done for. But raw fighting instinct refused to die. He raised himself on one elbow. Snarling, spitting blood, he managed to fire one shot. The bullet grazed Jack's leg, a red hot iron searing his skin.

Then Corcoran's second shot finished it. The bullet took away what was left of the marshal's face. It ripped down through his temple, tore an exit hole at the angle of his jaw. Fragments of bone gleamed white in the blood.

Then the blacksmith was there, running, breathless. One glance told him Jack Garrison was alive. He said, 'Raker's dead,' then took one look at the dead marshal, turned away, and brought up his breakfast.

NINETEEN

Phoenix, Arizona – One week later

'I think it's about time the senator for Arizona honoured the town of Sureño with his presence. Without the town knowing what's going on, of course.'

'Are you mad?'

'If you mean angry, no, not yet. If you mean insane, then the no is quite definite.'

Ella Rome had been away visiting her 90-year-old mother. She had returned to find a man in her husband's office she did not recognize. He was unshaven, his whiskers grey. His grey hair was long, lank, unwashed. He was dressed in worn, threadbare range clothes, a Stetson that had once been dove-grey but was now sweat-stained and bleached by years in the Arizona sun. His boots were down at heel, the leather faded and lined with age.

Around this man's waist there was a gunbelt. The six-gun in its holster hung low on his right thigh, and was secured there by a rawhide thong.

'If you'd looked like that when I met you,' Ella sneered, 'I would have turned around and walked away.'

'And missed all the good times, the rich times. For many years I was the man you see now, and was respected for it.'

'Or feared. By men who looked at you with loathing, before being shot with that gun you're now carrying.'

'Perhaps.'

'What's this in aid of?'

'Tony's been in Sureño for the past eight days. I've heard nothing. It's best I go like this, unrecognized—'

'Oh, God damn you, Jeff Rome.' Her face had paled.

'Don't think the worst, Ella. Over the years our son has proved he's well able to take care of himself.'

'But can you?'

Rome frowned. 'I don't understand. I'm wearing my six-gun, yes, but why should I be in any danger?'

'I'm not talking about Sureño.'

'Then…?'

'I'm giving you a warning,' Ella said. Her shoes tapped on the board floor as she crossed the room and poured herself a drink. The decanter rattled against the crystal glass. When she again turned to face him, her cheeks were flushed an angry red.

'If anything has happened to Tony,' she said, 'I will destroy you.'

His smile was sceptical. 'What, with the little pistol I bought so that you could protect your honour?'

'Oh no, if anything has happened to my boy then killing would be much too good for you.' And now Ella was smiling, but it was a smile of infinite cruelty. 'I will expose you, tell the whole truth about what happened when a train was robbed twenty years ago. How men obeyed your orders. How an innocent man went to jail. That's what I mean by destroying you. Because once that truth emerges, you will no longer be known as Senator Jefferson T. Rome. You'll be identified by a number, and for the rest of your life your home will be a bare cell in the Yuma state penitentiary.'

TWENTY

Seven days ago, three men had lain dead outside Elgan Lloyd's Tredegar ranch, on ground warmed by the sun yet chilled by the cooling flesh of men shot down in their prime. Jack's six-gun bullets had put one of the Phoenix marshals out of the fight. Corcoran's accurate rifle fire had ended Raker's short life as the town's marshal, then cut down the second Phoenix marshal to save Jack's life.

Old man Lloyd was so wasted his corpse was like a bundle of dry twigs inside old clothing. The head – though rarely active – of the small town council, he had been cynically shot down to prove a point to Jack Garrison. Because he had died on his own property, Jack and Corcoran had left him there. They'd hurriedly buried Raker and the two marshals on the other side of the trees lining the trail. When that was done they stripped the rigs from the three dead men's horses, dumped them by the fresh graves, and left the horses to graze.

Corcoran rode alone into Sureño and took it upon himself to inform the town council – without going into details – that two of their men had met violent deaths: their leader, and the new marshal who'd barely had time to pin on his badge. Lynch, the ailing deputy Jack had encountered in Mackie's saloon, had recovered from his fever and was immediately promoted to marshal. And, much to Corcoran's astonishment, old men with eyes showing weariness caused by the spate of deaths in a peaceful Arizona town had looked on him favourably and offered him the job of deputy.

Rick Garrison had been buried in a short evening ceremony at the town cemetery. Jack was an escaped convict. That naturally made showing his face in public a risk. Though it was unlikely that anybody other than those associated with the Lloyds knew he was back in his home town, he had decided it was best to watch from a stand of trees to the south of the old graveyard. That had been hard to bear but, because he and his brother had been apart for twenty years, there was more a vague sense of loss than of overpowering grief.

While watching that burial as the sun lengthened shadows cast by simple wooden crosses, old and new, Jack was more disturbed by the realization that Rick might have died for nothing. Raker was dead, and though the other three men involved in the train robbery – Geraint Lloyd, Ellis and Soames – were alive and kicking, they were of no concern to Garrison: he was of the opinion that without leadership they would back off, leave him alone.

But it was his firm belief that only Elgan Lloyd knew the name of the man behind the train robbery. Lloyd's death meant that Jack was no closer to that man's identity than he had been when he came over the penitentiary wall. And it was that problem that occupied his time before Ed Corcoran came bearing disturbing news.

There was a big, empty room above Ed Corcoran's workshop. The way in was by a rickety ladder with worn rungs that reached up to a plain wooden hatch. The room was dusty, festooned with cobwebs, bright daylight reduced to gloom by the years of filth coating the small window's panes.

Corcoran had stabled Jack's horse in the livery barn, paying in advance without mentioning an owner's name. Again, figuring it was best to stay hidden, the room above the workshop had become Jack's temporary home. The space was little better than his former prison cell. In the dead of the first night, Corcoran had climbed the ladder lugging a holed mattress trailing corn husks. Jack spent his days roasted by the sun beating down on the tin roof, the heat of the forge blasting through the warped, under-foot boards. At night, when the forge had cooled, he would shiver on the mattress, his only cover a thin horse blanket.

Corcoran brought a hot meal at the end of each day. In between times, Jack survived with a jug of water and a stub of candle.

And his banjo.

The rolled bandanna was once again behind the co-ordinator rods, rolled extra tight the further to reduce the sound. But there was little chance of his being heard. In daylight hours the town was a noisy bustle of activity. Throughout the day when he wasn't occupied by his work as deputy marshal, the clanging of Corcoran's hammer was loud enough to turn men deaf. In the hours of darkness the only sounds came from the creatures of the night: bats, hunting owls, the screech of a fox, the mournful howl of a coyote.

So Jack Garrison played his banjo, gently and repeatedly plucking the five strings, coaxing from the ancient instrument the old tunes, the familiar tunes, the jigs and reels and haunting songs of love he had played throughout the long years of an imprisonment that might have driven other innocent men insane.

He was so engaged – and yet again wondering what the hell he could do to break the impasse – when the hatch was pushed open and Corcoran stepped in off the ladder.

'He's getting on in years,' Corcoran said. 'Worn range clothes. Lank grey hair. An air of world weariness, rides a tired-looking nag. What does that suggest?'

'A saddletramp, a range drifter, making one more stop in one more town?'

'That was the impression I got, almost dismissed him as of no importance,' Corcoran said. 'Trouble is, the man's eyes tell a different story.'

He'd climbed the ladder using one hand. In the other he held a bottle of whiskey. Now he splashed drinks into two shot glasses he took from the pockets of his leather vest, his movements causing the light from the candle to glint in the deputy's badge.

'Been stealing from Mackie's?'

'Borrowed. Beats drinking from the bottle.'

'This drifter's eyes?'

'Intelligent. Guarded. He's up to something. He headed straight for the jail, spoke to Lynch. Don't ask me what was said, and there's nothing to be gained by going in there and asking Lynch.'

'You're Lynch's deputy. You have a right to know, he has a duty to keep you informed.'

'If there was a book of instructions on how to behave as town marshal, no doubt Lynch would follow it to the letter. No such screed exists, so he's all puffed up with power and making his own rules.'

'Then we're no further forward?'

'We'll come to that shortly,' Corcoran said, 'but there's something else I can tell you for sure. The man who came out of the jail was a different feller from the one that went in.'

'Different how?'

'The guard had slipped, there was anger in his eyes. No, stronger than that, fury, only barely held back on a very tight rein. Came out onto the plank walk like a man with a mission. Looked around him with such blazing intensity that passing folk sheered off and gave him a wide berth.'

Jack tasted his drink. 'A lot of men recently dead,' he said. 'If he was asking the right questions, this wayfarin' stranger will have got names from Lynch. Be a help if we knew why, and which name lit the fuse.'

'You spent twenty years plucking a banjo in an empty room. I spent the first five of those years in Phoenix. The man most often had his name printed bold in Phoenix newspapers was a feller called Rome.'

Jack stared. 'Same as the lawman who met sudden death. You saying those Romes are related? OK, let's say this drifter's the dead lawman's pa. He'll be looking for the killer. That's understandable; any father would do the same. It maybe puts me in more danger – or was it you killed Rome? – but doesn't get us any closer to the man behind the train robbery, the cruel hanging of your pa.'

'I reckon you're wrong.' There was a devilish light in Corcoran's eyes. 'That feller called Rome who had his name in those Phoenix papers was the state senator. Was, and is now. Jefferson T. Rome. And this is what's significant, Jack: he was elected to office just a few weeks after you took up long-term residence in that one-room apartment in Yuma.'

'Jesus Christ,' Jack said. 'And you're sayin'…?'

'I'm saying this drifter, this wayfarin' stranger, is Senator Jefferson T. Rome. The politician's come a-hunting, and he's doing it himself because his whole future's at stake. He tried the other way, keeping his head down, and sent his son to do his dirty work. And, yes, his son was killed in a shootout. But much more important to Rome than any death in the family is finding the convict who came over a prison wall to threaten his career.'

TWENTY-ONE

Suspicion is not proof. Proving guilt in a politician who had served the state of Arizona with honour for the past twenty years would prove difficult, for anyone. For an escaped convict and a blacksmith recently turned deputy marshal, it would be nigh on impossible.

Frustration saw Jack Garrison and Ed Corcoran reaching for the whiskey bottle. An hour or so later Jack turned that empty bottle upside down, watched the drips with a poisonous gaze that had turned bleary, then flung the bottle furiously from him to shatter into a thousand glittering fragments against the loft wall.

They had talked and got nowhere. Weariness and a whiskey bottle sucked dry saw them devoid of ideas, without the clarity of thought needed to pursue the subject further. Corcoran slapped Jack's shoulder, then stumbled to the hatch and felt his way down the ladder. Jack fell onto the corn-husk mattress, stared at the room in the light of the guttering candle and felt defeat like an intolerable weight on shoulders that had borne too much for too long.

But the night wasn't over.

Corcoran made it down the ladder to his forge, but no further. And proof of a supposedly honourable man's guilt didn't need to be sought. It came at them out of the silvery moonlight, and it grabbed them by the throats in a hold that could only end in death.

Jack's head had scarce touched his hard pillow when he was jerked back to full wakefulness. Below, in the forge, a man roared in anger. The shout was chopped off. Iron clanged, there was a muffled thud. In his mind's eye Jack could see Corcoran confronted, felled by a vicious blow, dragging with him as he collapsed one of the heavy tools he had grabbed for a weapon. Even as those pictures flashed through his mind, Jack was rolling off the mattress, cursing the effects of too much whiskey as he reached with fumbling hands for his gunbelt.

Senator Jefferson Rome was too fast.

Moving with extraordinary speed for a man of his age, he reached the top of the ladder when Jack was sprawled on his face, his hands still reaching.

'Leave it.'

The words were punctuated by the sound of a big weapon being cocked. When Jack twisted his head he was looking at the drifter Corcoran had accurately described: a man with lank grey hair, a face with several days' growth of whiskers, blue eyes that showed intelligence, and, now, a gleam of confidence, and of triumph.

The twin barrels of a shotgun were rock steady. Jack

was staring into the weapon's yawning muzzles.

'We're going for a ride, Mister Garrison. You won't need your six-gun, not now, not ever.'

Jack rolled, sat up.

'Corcoran?'

'Fast asleep. I think it's what's called the sleep of the dead.'

'You son of a bitch.' Jack stared hard at the senator. 'Any objection to a man bringing his banjo?'

'None whatsoever. I'm partial to the instrument's melodic sound, though I doubt you'll have the opportunity or the time to entertain me.'

'You never know,' Jack said with a smile.

A swift roll brought him lithely to his feet. He slung the banjo over his shoulder by its plaited cord. The six-gun he left on the loft's floor. Rome preceded him down the ladder, but the shotgun never wavered from its target, and even in the gloom Jack was conscious of the senator's knuckles gleaming white on the double triggers.

It crossed his mind to slip deliberately, crunching down on several of the ladder's old rungs so that his full weight dropped onto the man with the gun and carried him all the way down to fall heavily on the workshop's dirt floor.

But Rome was ahead of him in his thinking. Jack was still calculating the risk involved when the senator dropped nimbly from the ladder and, grinning ferociously, stood well back with the raised weapon to watch from a safe distance as Jack climbed down.

Ed Corcoran was an inert figure lying flat on his back

close to the cold forge. His head was turned to the side, his cheek lying in a scattering of bloody ash and cinders. His eyes were closed, his face white, but in the quick glance he cast in the downed man's direction Jack saw the slow rise and full of the big man's chest.

'My horse—'

'Outside, ready,' Rome said. 'Nothing has been left to chance.'

'How did you find me?'

'Through Corcoran. I know that name only too well. Discovering that the son of a hanged man was a blacksmith and deputy marshal here in Sureño was a stroke of luck. I followed him here to his forge, watched and waited. My reward came when I saw the dim light in the window above the workshop. Drew the right conclusion, and bided my time. I'd figured that before too long Corcoran would come out. He had his back to me when he came down the ladder, moved fast for a big man when he realized the danger. But not fast enough.'

'And now?'

'I put right a mistake I made twenty years ago. Or, let me put it another way. All knots will be knotted, all loose ends securely tied.' Again he grinned. 'If you've learned anything at all since coming over the penitentiary wall, that statement will send a chill down your spine.'

TWENTY-TWO

Rome lashed Garrison's hands to the saddlehorn. He tied another rope to an ankle, passed it under Garrison's horse, and knotted it around his other ankle. Pulled it tight. The ropes bit into flesh. Already Garrison could feel his hands swelling, his feet turning numb.

They rode out of Sureño in an easterly direction. The night was moonlit, and cool, the dry Arizona terrain wiped clean of colour. The Gila River was an ever present silver ribbon, sometimes seen clearly, at other times as a shimmering light filtering through stands of wilting cottonwoods.

After ten miles of steady riding, Rome turned away from the river. He led the way across the shiny lines of the railroad – always riding off to one side so that he could keep an eye on his captive – and headed into an area of barren scrubland. Ahead of them were low hills, their ridges and crests outlined in the moonlight. They rode through areas of dry chaparral and greasewood, the moon lighting the low-lying manzanita, the tall Spanish daggers. Thin stands of blue Palo Verde could be seen spread across the steep slopes of canyons cutting into the higher ground, those groves becoming a little denser in the hollows where moisture lingered.

Hanging trees, Jack Garrison thought grimly, for Rome's message to him as they rode away from the unconscious Corcoran had been clear. Somewhere not too far ahead there would be a tree waiting patiently for a rope to be tossed over a stout bough, for a fourth man to die with bulging eyes and heels futilely kicking. At that point, for Jefferson Rome, an unfinished story would be brought to a close and the closing would see his career made safe.

But was this why he, Jack Garrison, had escaped from a prison cell?

Perhaps it was, he thought, feeling the first faint stirrings of hope as he glanced sideways at Jefferson Rome. Something about the senator suggested that before political life he had been a hard man, a man who rode a solitary trail where danger lurked. Yet here and now the past counted for nothing. Garrison noted the stiffness in the senator's back, a clear indication that the big man was beginning to realize the enormity of the task he had set himself. He was leading a man to death by hanging. The mere thought of what that entailed must be curdling his blood.

The Arizona senator had bought his position with money stolen from a train, and three men innocent of that crime had been hanged so that justice was seen to be done. But Rome had not soiled his hands; had not

152

tasted on dry lips the gunpowder that had ripped apart a railway carriage and torn the guards to bloody shreds; had not wielded the quirt that drove startled horses out from under those three doomed men with hollow, innocent eyes.

He had been far removed, perhaps in the state capitol arrogantly telling an astonished bank manager that his almost empty account would soon see an influx of funds, then going on to admire from a distance those offices that, if all went well, would soon be his to occupy. And, yes, everything had gone according to plan, Garrison thought – but what mattered now was that a man whose hands were soft and white from twenty years' riding a Phoenix desk was contemplating stringing up a desperate convict.

That the convict had also spent those years without wielding axe or spade, had almost forgotten what it felt like to hold taut reins in his gloved hands, was neither here nor there. It was the degree of desperation that would make a difference. Jefferson Rome was defending his reputation. Jack Garrison would be fighting for his life.

'*And that,*' Garrison whispered through clenched teeth, '*gives me the edge.*'

'You say something?'

'Praying,' Garrison said. 'You should do the same.'

'I've always admired optimism,' Rome said, 'but your thinking is flawed. You believe I'm a weak man not capable of stringing you up, but you're wrong.'

'I'll be watching with interest.'

'Not at first, you won't.' Rome shook his head. 'You're tied to that horse for a reason. You can't fall off. All I need do is club you unconscious. It's then a simple matter to put the noose around your neck, throw the end of the rope over a branch and pull it tight.'

'And then?'

'When you open your eyes and begin to watch, as you put it, with interest,' Rome said, 'I whip the horse out from under you, watch you die, then head for home.'

While talking they had moved off the indistinct trail. The horses were heading at a walk towards tall trees blanketing the lower slopes of a canyon. Guided by Rome, they pushed through silently; their hoofs were deadened by thick blankets of dead leaves. Less than a hundred yards into the trees they broke through thick, crackling undergrowth to emerge in a small clearing. The moon glinted on the pale bones of fallen men almost hidden in the long grass. Above them, three ropes dangled, their ends frayed and ragged.

'You know this place,' Garrison accused. 'You've been here before, and here's me thinking it was the Lloyds did your dirty work.'

'Some things,' Rome said, 'cannot be left to chance. I was here for the hangings, watching from the back of the room in Sureño when you were tried and convicted.'

'And then,' Garrison said softly, 'you rode home. As you will very soon, because you've planned this well.'

Rome rode in close to Garrison's roan, dragging his shotgun out of its leather boot. He hefted it in gloved hands. It was the weapon he would use as a club.

'Untie my hands.'

'What?'

'A dying man's final request,' Garrison said. 'Maybe I'm craving a last cigarette.

'You think I'm stupid? It's not a cigarette you crave, it's freedom—'

'You can tie them again when I'm finished.'

'Finished what?'

'You're right, it's not a cigarette. Banjo music saw me through twenty years of incarceration. It's only right that it should give me comfort now, ease my way to the afterlife.'

'There's no such thing,' Rome said bluntly. He hesitated, eyeing Garrison, looking for the trap. Then he swiftly drew a knife and leaned sideways out of the saddle to cut the rawhide binding Garrison's wrists.

'The unusual feature of this instrument,' Garrison said, rubbing life back into his hands then unslinging the banjo, 'is that the sound can be deadened – which is good for you, because you don't want me attracting attention.'

'This is an empty wilderness at the dead of night. Get on with it. Play your tune.' Rome laughed harshly. 'Something appropriate. Can you manage the funeral march?'

'Anything,' Garrison said, 'but first I've got something to show you.'

He grinned, then turned the banjo so that its open back was facing the senator. He pulled the rolled bandanna out from behind the co-ordinator rod. Held it up. Began to unroll the faded red cloth.

'The top's a resonator made of animal skin,' he said. 'Padding it with fabric stuffed behind the rod takes away the harsh sound, makes the music mellow.'

Still talking, telling a tale he had told to a bounty hunter who thought he was the best, Garrison fully unrolled the bandanna. Then, like a matador using his cape to torment the bull, he flapped the red cloth open and held it high and to one side.

Rome's eyes had instinctively followed the movement.

With all the strength of his right arm and shoulder, Garrison swung the long-necked banjo horizontally. The banjo was an axe. Garrison was a lumberjack, felling a tree. The five strings hummed in the air. The brass frets glittered in the moonlight. Rome saw the blow coming. In the fraction of a second left to him, his eyes dilated. Then the banjo hit him a terrible blow under his left ear. There was an audible crack as his neck snapped. The light in his eyes was extinguished. He toppled from his horse, and fell backwards into the long grass and the old and fragile bones of long dead men.

EPILOGUE

Jack Garrison was struggling to loosen the twisted rawhide thongs lashing his ankles when Ed Corcoran rode out of the trees and into the clearing. The blacksmith had dried blood on the side of his face. An ugly bruise painted his cheekbone purple. His right eye was swollen shut.

He was not alone.

The woman who rode a little way behind him on what looked like a fine thoroughbred mare wore elegant riding clothes. A silk scarf was wrapped around her neck, and lifted to cover her mouth. Her dark hair was streaked with grey. Already pale in the moonlight, her face turned chalk-white when she looked beyond the blacksmith and saw Rome lying crumpled amid old, broken bones.

'I wasn't thinking,' Garrison said angrily as Corcoran leaped from his horse and crouched to untie his ankles. 'I needed Rome alive to prove my innocence. Sure, I hit him ferociously because he was all set on stretching my neck. But a little thought would have seen me deliver a blow that knocked him unconscious. Now there's no way back for me.'

'Indeed there is,' the woman said softly.

'This is Ella Rome,' Corcoran said as Garrison slid from his horse, sank to the cool grass with his banjo cradled. 'She rode into town late, came all the way from Phoenix after her husband.'

'After my late husband,' she corrected. 'But you really don't need him,' she said to Garrison. 'In some ways I share his guilt. The least I can do is make recompense.'

'In that case, I'll ask you a question,' Garrison said. 'I'll do it using the weapon that saved my life.'

His fingers stroked the banjo's strings. He plucked a few single notes, played a sequence of melodic chords, and began softly to croon.

He sang *Skip to my Lou*. In that wan moonlight the song was haunting. He chose the verse that, in Mackie's saloon, had brought Joe Dublin's wrath down on his head.

Lost my partner. What'll I do?
Lost my partner. What'll I do?
Lost my partner. What'll I do?

And there he paused, and looked questioningly at Ella Rome.

Her smile was venomous.

'What I'll do,' she said, 'is ride with you into Sureño, then on to Phoenix. When I talk to the authorities there, your name will figure prominently, the pardon you deserve sure to follow when I begin dismantling the reputation of the late, unlamented, Jefferson T. Rome.'